Dear Reader,

This month is a very sp[...]
this being my first ever [...]
sixtieth birthday!

I'm thrilled to be part of the celebrations with *Surrender to the Playboy Sheikh*. Sixty years is an incredibly long time in publishing, and I'm so proud to be part of that history—especially as it's a milestone book for me, being my thirty-fifth!

I first discovered Harlequin when I was thirteen. I was always a bookworm and I always knew I wanted to be a writer, but it was reading Sara Craven's Harlequin Presents® novel *The Devil at Archangel* that made me realize I wanted to be a romance writer. What I loved about the book was the sparkling characterization, the great dialogue, the way that love overcame all the obstacles…and, most of all, the happy ending.

Fast-forward thirty years, and those elements are still at the core of Harlequin's books. Although the issues writers raise have changed—we write contemporary books that reflect our times—the important bits of the romance are still there. A hero you can fall in love with, a heroine you'd like to be (or be her best friend, maybe!) and the fact that you might go through difficult times, but there's always going to be hope and happiness at the end.

A Harlequin novel is the perfect rainy-day read, because it puts a bit of sunshine and sparkle into life and a smile on my face. It's also the kind of book I enjoy writing, because I love being able to give my readers that same warmth and sparkle.

Happy birthday, Harlequin. And here's to many more!

With love,

Kate Hardy

To Tame a *Playboy*

Hot, sexy and double the pleasure!

*Harlequin Presents® introduces
Kate Hardy's new playboy duet*

Look out for book two,
Playboy Boss, Pregnancy of Passion

Coming next month from Harlequin Presents®

Kate Hardy

SURRENDER TO THE PLAYBOY SHEIKH

To Tame a *Playboy*

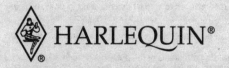

HARLEQUIN®

TORONTO • NEW YORK • LONDON
AMSTERDAM • PARIS • SYDNEY • HAMBURG
STOCKHOLM • ATHENS • TOKYO • MILAN • MADRID
PRAGUE • WARSAW • BUDAPEST • AUCKLAND

Recycling programs
for this product may
not exist in your area.

ISBN-13: 978-0-373-12841-9

SURRENDER TO THE PLAYBOY SHEIKH

First North American Publication 2009.

Copyright © 2009 by Pamela Brooks.

www.eHarlequin.com

Printed in U.S.A.

All about the author...
Kate Hardy

KATE HARDY lives on the outskirts of Norwich, England, with her husband, two small children, a dog—and too many books to count! She wrote her first book at age six when her parents gave her a typewriter for her birthday.

She had the first of a series of sexy romances published at twenty-five, and swapped a job in marketing communications for freelance health journalism when her son was born, so she could spend more time with him. She's wanted to write for Harlequin since she was twelve, and when she was pregnant with her daughter, her husband pointed out that writing medical romances would be the perfect way to combine her interest in health issues with her love of good stories.

Kate is always delighted to hear from readers. Do drop by her Web site at www.katehardy.com.

For Liz Fielding—whose friendship I appreciate as much as her books (and her gorgeous sheikhs!)—with love.

CHAPTER ONE

'THANK you so much for your time, Your Highness.' The journalist was practically curtseying to him. Something Karim really, really hated.

But he managed to stay polite. 'No problem. Nice to meet you.' He was aware that he was wearing just as false a mask as the journalist was.

No doubt she thought she had some great quotes to use in a diary piece. This was the kind of party that always made the gossip columns—high-level people from the business world, politicians and hotshot brokers and a sprinkling of actors and pop stars.

And he knew exactly what the spin was going to be where he was concerned. That His Royal Highness Karim al-Hassan had been partying hard, with a champagne reception every day for the last week and languorous lunch engagements that started before midday and never finished before three.

Five years ago, they might've been right. He'd partied with the best of them. Burned the candle at both ends.

But now…it was old news. Though in some respects it suited him—people were nowhere near as guarded with him when they thought he was just out for fun, a charming and sophisticated dilettante.

What the newspapers all missed was that Karim's glass usually held sparkling mineral water rather than gin and tonic.

That he had a retentive memory and didn't need to make notes—he could recall every detail of a meeting and follow it up with letters or reports as necessary. And none of them had any idea that when he left a lunch meeting or a party, he'd be working on complicated figures or reading reports from focus groups until the early hours.

Since his father had entrusted him with such an important task—developing tourism and foreign investment in Harrat Salma—Karim had been more businessman than playboy. He'd done the research, met the right people, made the right contacts, written his business plans. And now he needed to make the most of it. He'd set up a series of meetings with people he knew would bring in investment that would help create more jobs, better infrastructures and the chance to develop sustainable energy sources in his country. All of which would help put Harrat Salma at the forefront.

Even as he chatted pleasantly among a group of people, smiling and making appropriate comments in the right places to show he'd been listening, Karim's mind was working on his business plan. Though something nagged at him to turn round. Like a whisper in his head that wouldn't go away.

Eventually, he gave in.

Turned round.

The woman across the other side of the room caught his attention immediately, despite the fact that she was clearly dressed to be invisible rather than to shine. Her hair was an ordinary brown, caught back at the nape. Her black shift dress was simple, elegant and very plain. Her shoes were low-heeled, rather than strappy high heels. She wore no jewellery, not even a watch. No make-up, unless she'd gone for the 'barely there' look that he knew from experience was incredibly high maintenance—though, given the rest of her appearance, he didn't think so.

Odd.

She was the complete opposite of the women he usually

dated. Given that she'd dressed to be ignored, he shouldn't even have noticed her. Yet she was beautiful in her simplicity. And something about her drew him. As if there were some connection between them.

He'd never seen her before. He would've remembered her, he was sure. He had no idea who she was—but right at that moment he *really* wanted to know. And even though he was supposed to be networking, he could allow himself five minutes off. Just long enough to find out who she was and ask her out to dinner.

She was talking to Felicity Browne, the hostess. Karim quietly slipped away from the group and sauntered casually across the room towards the two women. When their conversation ended and she turned away, he quickened his pace slightly and intercepted her path. 'Hello.'

'Hello,' she said politely.

She had a faint South London accent, he noticed. And up close he could see that her eyes were a serious, quiet grey-blue.

Serious and quiet. *Definitely* not like the women he usually dated.

'You don't have a drink,' he said, shepherding her over towards a waiter bearing a tray of glasses.

'Because I'm not really here,' she said.

Although she was obviously aiming to sound cool and collected, Karim had trained himself to notice the little things—and he noticed that she was very slightly flustered.

Given that she'd been talking to Felicity, it was a fair bet that she was a member of Felicity's staff. So it followed that she was probably worried about getting into trouble for hanging around at a party she really wasn't dressed to attend—or invited to.

Well, he could fix that.

'Let's go somewhere quieter,' he said. 'I'll get you a drink first.'

'Thank you, but I don't drink.'

'Then have a mineral water.' He took two glasses from the waiter's tray and handed one to her. A quick check told him that the reporter had indeed left the party: good. Now he could relax. He tucked her free arm through his before heading for the French doors he knew led to a balcony.

Oh, help, Lily thought.

She'd only slipped into the room for a few moments—very quietly and discreetly—to check that Felicity was happy with everything. Then she'd intended to go straight back to the kitchen and sort out the puddings. She certainly hadn't intended to let herself be waylaid like this.

Even if he was the most stunning man Lily had ever seen.

He was dressed like the rest of the male guests, in a dinner suit teamed with a white, wing-collar pleated-front shirt. His black silk bow tie was hand-tied rather than ready-made. A swift glance at his highly polished black shoes told her that they were handmade, and the cut of the suit was definitely made-to-measure rather than off-the-peg. *Expensive* made-to-measure, judging by the feel of the cloth against her fingers. Everything about him screamed class.

Well, it would. Felicity Browne was posh with a capital P, and her guests were the same.

Lily had met a few of them before—cooked for them, even—but she'd never met him. She would've remembered. He had the same accent as most of the men in the room—one she recognised as public school followed by Oxbridge—and his almost black hair was cut slightly too long with a fringe that flopped over his eyes. Definitely an upper-class playboy.

Though his olive skin and amber-coloured eyes were just a touch too exotic for him to be English.

'I really shouldn't b—' she began again as he opened the French doors, guided her onto the balcony and closed the doors behind them.

'Don't worry. If Felicity says anything, I'll tell her I kidnapped you and it wasn't your fault,' he reassured her.

'But—'

'Shh.' He placed his forefinger against her lips, his touch gentle yet firm enough to tell her he meant it. No more protesting.

And then he held her gaze and traced the tip of his forefinger across her lower lip. The lightest, sheerest contact—and yet Lily couldn't move. Didn't want to move. There was something compelling about him, something that drew her to him. From the look in his eyes, she had a feeling it was exactly the same for him.

Instant attraction.

Spark to a flame.

A single touch would be enough to ignite it.

She should leave now. If she acted on her heart instead of her head, it would be a disaster. She couldn't afford the kind of gossip that would undoubtedly follow—gossip that would insidiously eat away at the foundations of the business she'd worked so hard to build, and bring it crashing down.

But, for the life of her, she couldn't walk away.

'What's your name?' he asked softly.

'Lily.'

'Karim,' he introduced himself.

Exotic—and yet he had that very English accent. Intriguing. And she wanted to know more.

'One question,' he said softly. 'Are you married, involved with anyone?'

She knew instinctively that if she said yes, he'd let her go. Then she could escape back to the kitchen. She actually considered lying to him; although dishonesty was something she usually despised, in this case she knew a white lie would be the most sensible course of action.

But her body wasn't listening to her head. She gave the tiniest, tiniest shake of her head, and saw relief bloom in his expression. Followed quickly by a hunger that made her body tighten in response.

He put his glass down on the table, then took hers from her hand and placed it next to his, all the while keeping his gaze fixed on hers. He captured her hand and raised it to his mouth; as he kissed each fingertip in turn she couldn't help her lips parting and her head tipping back slightly in offering.

He saw the invitation and took it, dipping his head so that his mouth just brushed her own. The lightest, sweetest, erotic whisper of skin against skin.

It wasn't enough.

She needed more.

Much more.

She slid her arms round his neck, drawing his head back down to hers. Even as she did it she knew it was crazy. They'd barely spoken a word to each other. Had only just exchanged first names. She didn't *do* things like this.

Yet here she was, kissing a complete stranger. A man she knew nothing about, except for his first name and the fact that he had the sexiest mouth she'd ever seen.

And then she stopped thinking as he deepened the kiss and her fingers tangled in his hair, urging him closer. His hair felt clean and springy under her fingers and she could smell the exotic scent of his aftershave, a sensual mixture of bergamot and citrus and amber. Simply gorgeous.

In turn, his arms were wrapped round her, one hand resting on the curve of her buttocks and the other flat against her back, drawing her closer against his body. So close that she could practically feel his heart beating, a deep and rapid throb that matched her own quickening pulse rate.

She'd heard people talking about seeing stars when they kissed and had always thought it an exaggeration. Now she knew exactly what they were talking about. This was like nothing else she'd ever experienced: as if fireworks were going off inside her head.

When he finally broke the kiss, she was shaking with need

and desire. Every nerve ending in her body was sensitised—and the sensation ratcheted up another notch when he traced a path of kisses along her jawbone to her ear lobe, and then another along the sensitive cord at the site of her neck. She shivered and arched against him; in response, he pulled her closer, close enough for her to feel his erection pressing against her belly. His palm flattened against her hip and stroked upwards, moulding her curves; when he cupped one breast, his thumb rubbing the hard peak of her nipple through the material of her dress, her knees went weak.

All her senses were focused on him. The tang of his after-shave, the more personal scent of his skin, the taste of his mouth on hers, the warmth of his hands through her clothes—a thin barrier that was suddenly way, way too thick for her liking. Right at that moment she really needed to feel his skin against hers. Soft and warm and incredibly sexy.

Then he went absolutely still. Lily opened her eyes and pulled back slightly, about to ask what was wrong, when she heard it, too.

The sound of a door closing.

People talking.

The chink of glasses.

Oh, Lord.

They weren't alone on the balcony any more. And she'd been so lost in the way he was kissing her…No doubt she looked as dishevelled as he did, with mussed hair and a mouth that was slightly reddened and swollen with kisses, making it obvious what they'd just been doing.

This was a disaster.

But hopefully it was fixable.

At least they weren't immediately in full sight; somehow while he'd been kissing her he'd managed to manoeuvre them behind one of the large potted palms at the side of the balcony, screening them from view.

Frantically, she smoothed her dress, removed the band keeping her hair tied and yanked her hair back into tight order. It was just as well they'd been interrupted, or who knew what they might have done?

She'd just broken every single one of her personal rules. Even though she'd hand-picked her staff and she knew they were perfectly capable of holding the fort, she should still have been there to oversee things and sort out any last-minute hitches. She was supposed to be *working*. And instead she'd let a complete stranger whisk her off to the balcony to kiss her stupid. She'd followed her libido instead of her common sense.

Had she really learned nothing from the wreck of her marriage?

Karim, too, was restoring order to his clothes.

'I really have to go,' she whispered, keeping her voice low so she wouldn't be overheard by the others on the balcony.

'Not yet,' he said, his voice equally soft. He traced the fullness of her lower lip with his thumb. 'Or I think both of us will be embarrassed.'

'But we didn't…' Lily's voice faded as a picture slammed into her mind—a picture of what would have happened if they hadn't been interrupted. A picture of him drawing the hem of her dress up around her waist while she undid his bow tie and opened his shirt. A picture of him lifting her, balancing her against the wall, and then his body fitting against hers, easing in and then—

'Don't,' he warned huskily, and she saw his pupils dilate. No doubt her thoughts had shown in her eyes, and he was thinking something along exactly the same lines.

All he had to do was dip his head slightly and he'd be kissing her again. Tasting her. Inciting her to taste him, touch him in return. And, Lord, she wanted to touch. Taste. Feel him filling her.

She swallowed hard.

Whatever was wrong with her? She never, but never, turned into a lust-crazed maniac. For the last four years she'd been single and perfectly happy with that situation. She had no intention of getting involved again. But this man had drawn an instant response from her. Made her feel the way nobody had before.

Which, as he was a total stranger, was insane.

This shouldn't be happening.

She only hoped the people who'd come out onto the balcony would go back into the main room again. The longer they had to stay behind the potted palm, the more embarrassing it would be when they finally emerged.

Again, his thoughts must have been in tandem with hers, because he said softly, 'The French doors are the only way out. Unless you're a gymnast in disguise and can launch yourself off the balcony onto a distant drainpipe, then shin down it.'

'Hardly. And I haven't been on a double-oh-seven training course,' she said ruefully, 'or I could've magicked a steel line from somewhere and clipped it onto the ironwork and we could both have abseiled down to the balcony beneath this one and escaped through the downstairs flat.'

'Great idea.' His eyes glittered with amusement. 'I wonder if my watch…?' He tapped it gently with his forefinger. 'Sadly, no. It's just a watch, I'm afraid. I didn't do the double-oh-seven training course, either.'

His teasing smile was the sexiest thing Lily had ever seen, and she almost—*almost*—found herself reaching up to pull his head back down to hers. But she managed to keep herself under control. Just.

'Looks like we'll have to wait it out, then,' she said quietly.

A wait that grew more and more awkward with every second; she didn't dare meet his eyes, not wanting him to guess how much she wanted him to kiss her again.

But then, at last, the hubbub of voices on the other side of the potted palms grew quiet and finally died away, followed by the distinct sound of the balcony doors closing.

Alone again.

And although the feeling of danger should've vanished with the people who'd left the balcony, Lily discovered that it had actually increased.

'Just for the record,' she said, 'I don't do this sort of thing.'

He gave her a rueful smile. 'I had intended just to introduce myself and ask you to have dinner with me.'

The 'but' hung in the air between them.

Instant attraction, that neither of them had been able to fight. Oh, Lord.

What if there had been problems? What if someone had come looking for her in the space of time she'd been out here with Karim, failed to find her, panicked?

She couldn't *afford* to do this. For her business's sake.

'I really do have to go,' Lily said.

He took a pen and a business card from his pocket, and scribbled a number on the back of the card. 'Call me,' he said, handing the card to her.

It was more of a command than a question. Karim was clearly a man who was used to people doing what he told them to. Normally, the attitude would have annoyed her. But that connection between them, and the way he'd kissed her... This sort of thing didn't happen every day. She had a feeling it had shaken him just as much as it had shaken her. And even though her head told her that this was a seriously bad idea, that relationships just messed things up and were more hassle than they were worth, her mouth had other ideas. 'I'll call you,' she agreed softly.

He cupped her face briefly with one hand, the gesture cherishing. 'Go,' he said. 'I'll stay here for a few minutes. And if Felicity isn't happy, text me and I'll go and talk to her.'

And charm her out of a bad mood, no doubt, Lily thought wryly. Not that she was going to let him make excuses for her. If there was a problem, it was her responsibility and she'd deal with it. But she knew he'd meant well, so she smiled politely. 'Thanks.'

As if he couldn't help himself, he brushed his mouth over hers. 'Later.'

And the promise in his voice sent another kick of desire through her.

CHAPTER TWO

'LILY! Oh, thank God you're back.' Beatrice, her chief waitress, sounded heartfelt.

'What's…? Oh.' Lily cut off the question, seeing Hannah, her assistant, clearing up a soggy mess from the floor. The bite-sized pavlovas topped with a slice of strawberry and a kiss of cream that she'd assembled fifteen minutes or so ago had turned into Eton Mess, splattered across the floor. The whole lot would have to go straight in the bin.

And now they were one large platter short of puddings.

Just as well that, knowing how easily meringues could shatter, Lily had brought extra to cover any breakages.

'Can you whip me some cream, Hannah?' she asked. 'And, Bea, if you can wash up that platter, please?' Meanwhile, she checked what she had left in the way of fruit. There weren't enough strawberries to do a full platter of mini strawberry pavlovas, but she could add some lemon curd to half the cream and add a slice of kiwi fruit for contrasting colour.

'I'm so sorry, Lily,' Hannah said, looking tearful. 'I wasn't looking where I was going, I tripped, and I—'

'Hey, no use crying over spilt meringues,' Lily interrupted with a smile. 'It happens. I have spares. It's fixable.'

'But…'

'It's *OK*,' Lily said, firmly yet gently. She knew exactly

why Hannah was distracted. Hannah's marriage was coming to a very messy end and the strain of trying to minimise the effects on her four-year-old daughter while trying to keep her life together was spilling over into her work. Not that Lily intended to read the Riot Act. Hannah, despite having a newborn, had been there for her when things had gone so badly wrong with Jeff. This was Lily's chance to do the same for her friend.

Jeff.

A harsh reminder of exactly why Lily shouldn't ring the number scribbled on the back of Karim's business card. Relationships spelled trouble. They distracted you from your goals and made life difficult. Particularly when your judgement in men was so lousy that you trusted them completely and they took advantage of your naivety. Took everything, the way Jeff had. Crushing her self-respect, her pride and her bank account. The sense of betrayal, hurt and loss had been crushing. And someone as gorgeous as Karim would have women dropping at his feet—just like Jeff. OK, she knew that not all men were unfaithful, lying louses…but Jeff had hurt Lily enough to make her extremely wary of relationships.

Pushing both her ex-husband and the gorgeous stranger out of her mind, Lily applied herself to assembling another plateful of pavlovas.

Working rapidly, she moved on to filling tiny choux buns with the coffee liqueur mousse she'd made earlier and sent Hannah out with a tray of miniature chocolate muffins and Bea out with melon-ball-sized scoops of rich vanilla ice cream covered in white chocolate and served on a cocktail stick.

The platters all came back with just a couple of canapés left on each. Good. She'd judged the quantities just right: enough to leave Felicity's guests replete but not enough to be wasteful. Years of having to struggle to pay off the overdraft Jeff had run up in her name—an overdraft he'd spent on his mistress—

meant that Lily absolutely loathed waste. Quietly pleased, she concentrated on clearing up.

She'd just finished when Felicity Browne came in. 'Lily, darling, that was stupendous.'

'Thank you.' Lily had learned not to protest that no, no, she was just average. There was no room for false modesty, in business. She wanted her clients to feel reassured that they'd made the right choice in using Amazing Tastes for their catering needs, and accepting their compliments helped to do that.

'Those little choux buns…' Felicity began wistfully.

Lily smiled, guessing exactly what Felicity wanted. 'I'll send you the recipe. And you don't have to make the choux pastry if that's a hassle for you. You can serve the mousse on its own, in little coffee cups—just garnish them with a couple of chocolate-covered coffee beans and maybe a sprig of mint for colour.'

Felicity laughed. 'That's exactly why I always ask you to do my parties. You're so good at those little extra touches.'

'Thank you.' Lily acknowledged the compliment with a smile.

She stayed just long enough to make the polite social chat she knew was expected of her, made one last check that she'd left Felicity's kitchen completely spotless, then dropped Hannah at her house on the way home. As she took her equipment out of the van and put it away Lily couldn't help thinking about Karim. And even though she knew it was crazy and it was way too late to call him, she fished inside her handbag for his business card.

Though it wasn't in the little pocket where she usually kept business cards. Odd. She'd developed a habit of filing things away neatly—they were easier to find, that way.

She checked the rest of her bag. It wasn't there, either.

Impossible. She was *sure* she'd put it in her bag.

And then she thought back. When she'd returned to the mini-crisis in the kitchen, she'd probably put the card on the worktop instead of her handbag, knowing that before she did anything else she needed to reassure her staff and stop them panicking.

Which meant that the card had probably been swept up with the refuse and thrown away.

Damn, damn, damn.

She could hardly phone Felicity and ask if she could rummage through the bin. And she definitely couldn't ask her for Karim's number or the guest list, because that would be completely unprofessional and Elizabeth Finch was never, but never, unprofessional.

Well, OK, *occasionally* she acted unprofessionally. As she had on a certain balcony, a couple of hours earlier that evening, when she'd kissed a tall, dark, handsome stranger. Really kissed him. And if they hadn't been interrupted, who knew what would have happened?

But it was over now.

Which she knew was for the best. Karim and his exotic amber eyes had tempted her to break all her personal rules. Losing his card had done her a favour—it had saved her from herself.

Karim was working through a set of figures when his phone rang. He answered it absently. 'Karim al-Hassan.'

'Your Highness, it's Felicity Browne. I wanted to thank you for these gorgeous roses.'

'My pleasure,' he said. He'd sent Rafiq, his assistant, to deliver a bouquet thanking her for her hospitality, along with a handwritten note of thanks. 'And please call me Karim.' He didn't insist on using his title in England, preferring people to be more relaxed with him.

'Karim,' she repeated obediently. 'Hardly anyone even writes a note nowadays, let alone sends such a lovely gift, especially on a Sunday,' she continued. 'Anyway, I won't keep you—I'm sure you're busy. But I couldn't just take these flowers for granted.'

He smiled. 'I'm glad you liked them. Actually, I had planned to call you later today.' He'd discovered this morning that he had a problem, and he hoped that Felicity would be able to give him a quick solution. 'The food last night was fabulous.'

'Thank you. But I'm afraid I can't take the credit for anything other than choosing the menu, and even in that I think I was guided,' Felicity admitted with a little laugh.

'Your staff?' he asked.

'Sadly not—it's a catering firm, Amazing Tastes.'

A very accurate name, Karim thought.

'I've asked Elizabeth Finch—the owner—several times if she'd come and work for me, offered her stupendous amounts of money, but she won't let anyone tie her down. I was lucky she could fit me in, because she's usually booked up for months in advance,' Felicity confided.

So the cook was freelance. Good. That meant there wouldn't be a problem asking her to cater for his presentations. Even though Felicity would probably have allowed him to poach her personal cook for a few days, this avoided any awkward obligations.

'Actually, I'm looking for a good caterer for some business presentations.' He'd had a caterer lined up. But as her sister had had a baby that morning, two months early, Claire had phoned him in a panic, saying that she needed to drop everything and look after her niece while her sister spent all her time at the special care baby unit. Except Claire's sister lived in Cornwall, a good five hours away—and as Claire was her only family, there was nobody else to do it.

He knew what it was like when family needed you to drop everything. He'd done it himself. So, although it left him in a jam, he wasn't going to give Claire a hard time about it. He still had enough time to fix things. 'I wondered if I could trouble you for your caterer's contact details?' he asked.

'Of course, but, as I said, she's very in demand,' Felicity warned. 'Though if she can't fit you in she might be able to suggest someone. She's good like that.'

Better and better.

'Let me get my contact book.' There was a pause; then Felicity dictated Elizabeth Finch's phone number and address.

Karim scribbled it down as she spoke. 'Thank you, Felicity.'

'My pleasure. And thank you again for the flowers.'

When he replaced the receiver, he flicked onto the Internet and looked up the address. Islington. A nice part of it. So she'd have a price tag to match.

Though money wasn't an issue. He needed quality—and he'd tasted that for himself, the previous evening. He glanced at his watch. Right now, a busy freelance caterer would be smack in the middle of preparations for an evening event, so this wasn't the best time to discuss a booking. He'd call in tomorrow at nine; from experience, he knew that face-to-face meetings were more effective than phone calls.

He glanced at his watch. Two hours, and he'd need to shower and shave and change for a garden party. A party that Renée, one of his prettiest recent dates, would also be attending. Given that the weather was fine and the garden in question had some nice secluded spots, it could be an interesting afternoon. A pleasant interlude.

Though, strangely, it wasn't Renée's face in his thoughts as he imagined kissing her stupid in the middle of the maze. It was Lily's.

He shook himself. It was highly unlikely that Lily would be there. And besides, now he thought about it, dating her would be too complicated. There had been something serious about Lily, and he wasn't in a position to offer anything serious. In less than a year's time he'd be back in Harrat Salma and his parents would be expecting to arrange a marriage exactly like their own. These were his last few months of playing. Of dating women who knew the score and didn't expect him to change his mind.

And he had no intention of changing that.

* * *

The next morning, Lily was sitting in her kitchen, drinking coffee and planning menus for the following week's events, when her doorbell buzzed. Too early for the postman, she thought, and she wasn't expecting any deliveries that morning. She wasn't expecting any visitors, either.

She opened the front door and stared.

Karim was the last person she'd expected to see. She'd only told him her first name—and it was her nickname rather than her full name. How come…?

'Lily?' he asked, looking as surprised as she felt. 'Do you work for Elizabeth Finch?'

She shook her head. 'I *am* Elizabeth Finch.'

He frowned. 'You told me your name was Lily.'

'It is.'

He looked sceptical, as if he wasn't sure she was telling the truth.

She shrugged. 'I couldn't say Elizabeth when I was tiny— I called myself "Lily-ba". The name kind of stuck. Everyone calls me Lily. Though obviously I use my full name for work.'

'I see.' He inclined his head. 'I was impressed by the food on Saturday night. I asked Felicity Browne for her caterer's contact details.'

Then this was a business call, not a social visit. Good. Business made things easier. She could section off her emotions and deal with this. Even better: if he became her client, that would be yet another reason not to act on that attraction. She knew first-hand that relationships and business didn't mix. Lord, did she know that first-hand. She'd been there already with Jeff and had her fingers well and truly burned. 'Come through.' She ushered him into the hall, closed the door behind him and led him through to the kitchen. 'Would you like some coffee?'

'Thank you. That would be nice.'

'Milk? Sugar?'

'Neither, thanks.'

'I'll put the kettle on. Do take a seat.'

At her gesture, Karim took a seat on one of the over-stuffed sofas set in the open-plan conservatory area, while Lily busied herself making fresh coffee. Her kitchen was clearly a professional kitchen—very up to date appliances, sleek minimalist units in pale wood, a central island, and what looked like granite work surfaces and splashbacks. Everything was neat and tidy, including the shelf of cookery books and box files. He wasn't surprised that she was the meticulous type.

And yet the room was far from sterile. The walls were painted a pale terracotta, adding warmth to the room, and there were photographs and postcards pinned to the fridge with magnets. A simple blue glass vase full of daffodils sat on the window sill behind the sink. And he could smell something gorgeous; a quick scan of the room showed him a couple of cakes cooling on a wire rack. For a client? he wondered.

Lily herself was dressed casually in jeans and a camisole top, and looked incredibly touchable. He could remember the softness of her skin against his and the sweetness of her scent when'd he kissed her on the balcony the other night, and his body reacted instantly.

Not good.

This was meant to be business. He knew that mixing business and pleasure wasn't a good idea—he needed to get himself under control again. Right now. He really shouldn't be thinking about hooking a finger under the strap of her top, drawing it down, and kissing her bare shoulder.

'Nice kitchen,' he commented when she returned with two mugs of coffee.

'It suits me,' she said simply.

And she suited it, he thought.

'So what did you want to discuss?' she asked.

She'd made quite sure she was sitting on the other sofa

rather than next to him, he noted. Fair enough. This was business. And sitting next to each other would've risked them accidentally touching each other. Given how they'd both gone up in flames the other night at the first touch, distance was a very good idea.

'As I said, I was impressed by the food at Felicity's party. I'm holding a series of business meetings and I need a caterer.'

'And you want m— You're asking me?' she corrected herself hastily.

A little slip that told him her mind was still running along the same track as his. 'Yes.' To both, he added silently.

'That depends when you have in mind. I'm booked up for the next three months.'

'They're set up for the end of the month.'

She shook her head. 'In that case, sorry, no can do.'

He backtracked to what she'd just said. 'You're working every single day for the next three months?' And people called *him* a workaholic.

'All my work days are booked.'

He picked up the subtext. 'So you don't work every single day.'

'Actually, I do,' she corrected. 'But I don't cook for other people every single day.'

'What do you do on the days you're not cooking for other people?'

'I develop recipes. I have a column in a Sunday newspaper twice a month, and a monthly column in a magazine.'

He couldn't resist. 'Are they work in development?' He gestured in the direction of the cakes.

'Is that a hint?'

He smiled. 'Yes.'

She rolled her eyes but, as he'd hoped, she smiled. 'OK. I'll cut you a slice. But be warned that it's a test, so it might not taste quite right.'

When she handed him a slice of chocolate cake on a plain

white plate, he took a mouthful. Savoured the taste. 'Works for me.' Though such a vague compliment would sound like flattery—something he knew instinctively she'd scoff at. 'It smells good and it's got the right amount of chocolate. Enough to give it flavour but not so much that it's overpowering.'

She tried it, and shook her head. 'The texture's not quite right. It needs more flour. Excuse me a minute.' She scribbled something on a pad.

'Notes?' he asked.

'For the next trial,' she explained.

He nodded in acknowledgement. 'So, to return to our discussion. Basically you have how many free days a week?'

'I have three days when I don't cook but they are my development time. Not to mention testing the recipes three times and setting up my kitchen so the photographer can take shots of the different stages. And time to do my paperwork.'

'But they're days you could use—in theory,' he persisted.

'In theory. In practice, I don't. If I do it for one person, I'll have to do it for everyone, and I don't want to end up working eighteen-hour days to fit everything in. I need time to refill the well. Time to let myself be creative.'

He tried another tack. 'You have people working for you, don't you?'

'Part time, yes.'

'But you've worked with them for a long time.'

She looked surprised. 'How did you know?'

'Because everything was so polished at Felicity's party. That kind of teamwork only comes with experience, when you know each other and trust each other.'

She recognised the compliment and smiled.

'And your staff help with the cooking?'

'Some of it.' She frowned. 'Why?

'I was thinking. Maybe you could delegate more to them.

Then you could expand your business without encroaching on the days you don't cook for people.'

She shook her head. 'Absolutely not. My clients expect my personal attention, and that's exactly what they get. The only way I can expand is if I get a time machine or a clone—neither of which are physically possible. I'm at capacity, Karim. Sorry. The best I can do is put you in touch with some of the people I trained with who also run their own businesses—they're good, or I wouldn't recommend them.'

This was where he knew he should be sensible, thank her for the recommendations, and call each one in turn until he found someone who could fit him in.

The problem was, he didn't want just anyone. He wanted *her*.

And he was used to getting exactly what he wanted.

'Thank you,' he said, 'but no. I want Elizabeth Finch.' He paused. 'Would any of your clients consider rescheduling?'

'No. And don't suggest I throw a sickie on them, either,' she warned. 'I'd never cheat my clients.'

'Good,' he said. 'You have integrity. I respect that.' He paused. 'Whatever your usual rates are, I'm happy to double them.'

'No.'

'You want to negotiate?' He shrugged. 'Fine. Let's save us both some time. Name your price, Lily.'

She folded her arms. 'You honestly believe everything can be bought?'

'Everything has a price.'

She scoffed. 'You must have a seriously sad life.'

He laughed. 'On the contrary. But it's basic business sense. Someone sells, someone buys. The price is negotiable, depending on supply and demand.'

'You can't buy people, Karim.'

He rolled his eyes. 'I know that. I'm not asking to buy *you*.' He paused just long enough for the colour to flood her face completely. 'In business, I look for the best. That's why I'm asking you to do the catering for some meetings that are going to be pretty crucial to *my* business.'

'I'm flattered that you've sought me out,' she said, 'but, as I've told you plenty of times already, I'm afraid I'm already booked and there's nothing I can do about it.'

'Firstly,' he said, 'persistence is a business asset. And, secondly, there's always a way round things if you look.'

'Hasn't anyone ever said no to you?'

He didn't even need to think about it. 'I always get what I want in the end.'

'Not in this case, I'm afraid. Unless you're prepared to take my next open slot, in three months' time.'

'I can't wait that long. The meetings are already set up.'

'Then, as I said, I'm sorry.' She went over to her filing system, took a box down, and made notes on a pad. She tore off the sheet, then brought it over to him. 'Here. They all come with my recommendation—and I'm picky.'

'So,' he said, 'am I.' He drained his mug. 'Thank you for the coffee. And the cake.'

'Pleasure.'

She was being polite, and he knew it. He also knew that if he gave in to the impulse to pull her to her feet and kiss her stupid, he'd push her even further away—she'd respond, but she'd be angry with herself for acting unprofessionally. And he wanted her willingly in his bed.

'If you change your mind—' and he had every intention of making sure that she did '—call me. You have my card.'

'Actually, I mislaid it.'

Had she? Or had she ripped it up in a fit of temper? Because now he knew exactly what she'd been doing at Felicity Browne's party, he could guess at her reaction that night after she'd left the balcony—anger at herself for letting him distract her when she'd been there in a business capacity. And underneath that cool, quiet exterior lurked a passionate woman. A woman who'd responded to him so deeply that they'd both forgotten where they were.

He took a business card from a small silver holder, scribbled his personal number on the back, and handed it to her. 'To replace the one you…' he paused, his eyes challenging hers '…mislaid.'

She didn't flinch in the slightest; she merely inclined her head in acknowledgement, and went back over to her filing system. She glanced at the name on the card, then paperclipped it into a book. Then she took a card from a box and handed it to him. 'In case you change your mind about the dates. But please remember that I have a three-month waiting list.'

'People plan parties that far in advance?'

'Weddings, christenings, anniversary dinners…' She spread her hands. 'I don't question my clients' social lives. I just talk to them about what kind of thing they want, and deliver it.'

'So you do dinner parties as well?'

'On Thursdays to Sundays,' she confirmed.

'And what if one of your regular clients needed you on a Monday, Tuesday or Wednesday?' he asked. 'Or they just decide to throw a party on the spur of the moment?'

'My clients know that I don't cook for people on Mondays, Tuesdays or Wednesdays. Apart from the fact that I have other commitments, everybody needs time off.'

'True.' That, together with her comment about a time machine, had just given him another idea. 'Well, it was good to see you again, Lily.'

'And you.'

For a moment, he thought about kissing her on the cheek— but he knew he wouldn't be able to leave it there. And he needed the business side of things sorted out before he addressed the issues between them. Before he took her to bed.

He knew that kissing her hand would be way too smarmy, so he settled for a firm handshake. 'Thanks for your time.'

Even something as impersonal as a handshake made his skin tingle where she touched him. And, judging by the look in her eyes—a look she masked quickly—it was the same for her.

This wasn't over.

Not by a long, long way.

CHAPTER THREE

'YOU, my friend, are just piqued. For the first time in your life, a woman has actually turned you down,' Luke said with a grin.

'I'm not piqued,' Karim said.

'You're distracted. Otherwise you'd have given me a better game tonight.'

Karim couldn't argue with that. Usually their Monday night squash matches were incredibly close, and tonight he'd lost badly. But he could argue with his best friend's earlier statement. 'Anyway, she didn't turn me down.'

Luke raised an eyebrow. 'I thought you just told me she was too busy to do the catering for your business meetings?'

'Kick a man when he's down, why don't you? Anyway, she'll change her mind.' Karim had every intention of changing it for her.

'Maybe I can help,' Luke suggested. Karim had explained the situation to him before the match. 'Cathy has some great ideas about revamping the café here—if you ask her nicely I'm sure she can come up with some menus for you and organise the catering. If it helps you out of a hole, she can use the kitchens here to sort out whatever you need done.'

'You'd let me poach your staff?' Karim asked. Luke had bought the health club three months ago and was in the process of making it reach its proper potential—a gym and spa bursting with vitality and an excellent café.

'Borrow. Temporarily. To help you out,' Luke corrected.

'But you'd want advertising or something in return.'

'I'm not *that* much of a shark. And I wouldn't make an offer like that to just anyone.' The corner of his mouth twitched. 'But I've just thrashed you at squash. And you're my best mate. So, as I'm feeling terribly sorry for you right now, you should take advantage of my good nature.'

Karim laughed. 'Ha. You wait until next Monday. I'll have my revenge.'

'In your dreams,' Luke teased back. 'Come on. We're both disgustingly sweaty and smelly—if we hang around here, bickering, we'll put off all my customers.'

'Whatever you say, boss.'

After a shower, they grabbed a cold beer in the bar.

'You're still brooding,' Luke said.

Karim made light of it. 'Just sulking about losing a match to you for the first time in a month. And by such a huge margin.'

'Are you, hell. You don't waste energy being competitive over something unimportant.' Luke paused. 'She must be really special.'

'Who?'

'The woman you're brooding about. Let me guess. Five feet eight, blonde, curvy and just lurrrves parties?'

Karim laughed dryly. 'That's your type, not mine.'

Luke grinned back. 'Don't kid yourself. I go for brunettes. Preferably ones without wedding bells in their eyes.'

And just in case they developed wedding bell-itis, as Luke had dubbed it, nobody ever made it to a fourth date.

'Actually, she's nothing like the type I usually date,' Karim said thoughtfully. 'Try five feet four, mid-brown hair and very hard-working.'

Luke blinked. 'You're kidding.'

'I wish I was. If she were a party girl, I'd know what made her tick. Lily…' Karim blew out a breath. 'She's different.' And maybe that was why he couldn't get her out of his head.

'And she's the caterer you want to work for you?' Luke queried.

'She cooks for the rich and famous. Hand-picked client list.' Karim leaned back against the leather club chair. 'She's the best. And I tasted her food at Felicity Browne's do, the other night, so I know what I'm talking about.'

He'd tasted her, too…and he wanted to do it again. And again. A lot more intimately.

Luke wrinkled his nose. 'I don't like the sound of this. Mixing business and pleasure—it never works, Karim. It'll end in tears. I've seen it happen too many times before.'

'Maybe.'

'*Definitely.*' Luke raised an eyebrow. 'So what's the plan?'

'I'm going to persuade her to change her mind.'

'You're going to charm her into working for you?'

Karim shrugged. 'I offered to pay her double. She just said that you couldn't buy people.'

'Too right. If you can buy them, they're not worth having around. They'll be unreliable.' Luke frowned. 'And if she drops clients in favour of you, what's to stop her dropping *you* if she gets a better offer?'

'I don't expect her to ditch long-standing arrangements in favour of me—and she told me up front she had no intention of dropping any of her clients for me. But I also happen to know there are three days a week when she doesn't have bookings. I want her on those three days.' Karim turned his glass of mineral water round in his hands. 'So it's a matter of getting to know her better. Finding out what's important to her. And then…negotiating terms.'

'It still sounds to me as if you're planning to mix business and pleasure. If you're going to be her boss, it's practically harassment,' Luke pointed out.

'She's her own boss. Technically, I'd be her client.'

'Same difference. Let it go,' Luke said. 'Sure, you're attracted to her. But there's a lot riding on these meetings. Screw it up for the sake of—what, half a dozen dates, before you get bored or she gets too serious and you back off?—and you'll never forgive yourself.'

'I'm not going to screw it up.'

'You will do, if you're thinking with another part of your anatomy instead of with your head,' Luke advised. He finished his drink. 'Think about what I said. If you want me to have a word with Cathy, let me know. It's not a problem.'

'Thanks. I appreciate the offer.'

There was a tinge of sympathy in Luke's eyes. 'It's tough, living up to a parent's expectations.'

Not as tough as having no family at all—though Karim didn't say so, knowing just how sensitive his best friend was about the issue. Particularly as Luke had been the one to walk away. 'I always knew I'd have to grow up and pull my weight in the family firm some time.' He just hadn't expected it to be this way. He'd seen himself in a supporting role, not the limelight.

But all that had changed five years ago when his brother had died. The whole world had turned upside down. So he'd done the only thing possible: given up his PhD studies and gone home to do his duty as the new heir to the throne.

A duty he still wasn't quite reconciled to. Not that he'd ever hurt his parents by telling them how he felt; and he would never, ever let them or his country down. But no matter how hard he worked or played, he still missed the studies he'd loved so much. Filling his time didn't fill the empty space inside him.

Karim finished his own drink. 'I've done quite enough loafing around for today. I'll see you later.'

'You're going home to work?'

Karim laughed as he stood up. 'Says the man who's going to do exactly the same thing.' Their backgrounds were miles apart, but Karim thought that he and Luke had a very similar outlook on life. They'd met on the first day of their MBA course, liked each other immediately, and the liking had merged into deep friendship over the years. Karim thought of Luke as the brother he no longer had, and Luke was the only person Karim would ever have talked to about Lily. And even though part of him knew that Luke was right, that mixing business and pleasure would lead to an unholy mess, he couldn't stop himself thinking about her.

By the time he'd walked home, he'd worked out what to do. There was something more important than money: time. And maybe that was the key to Lily. For the next couple of weeks, his work was flexible. He could fit in the hours whenever it suited him.

So maybe, just maybe, he had a way to convince her.

The following morning, he leaned on Lily's doorbell at nine o'clock sharp.

She opened the door and just stared at him for a moment.

And he was very, very aware that her gaze had gone straight to his mouth.

With difficulty, he forced his thoughts off her mouth and what he wanted to do with it. 'Good morning, Lily.'

'Good m—' she began, then frowned. 'What are you doing here?'

'I'm your new apprentice.'

She shook her head. 'Apart from the fact I already have all the staff I need, you can't be my apprentice—you don't have catering experience and you don't have a food hygiene certificate.'

'And how do you know that?' he challenged.

'I looked you up on the Internet.' She paused before adding, 'Your Highness.'

She'd looked him up. Just as he'd looked her up, the previous day. On her own website as well as the gossip pages.

Nobody had been linked with Lily's name for the last four years—probably, he thought, because she'd been too busy setting up and then running her business to socialise. Which suited him fine.

He met her gaze. 'And that's a problem?'

'If you think I'm going to let my clients down in favour of you just because you've got a title, then I'm afraid you'll be disappointed, Your Highness.'

He smiled, pleased that she had principles and stuck to them. 'My title has nothing to do with it. To you, I'm Karim.'

'*Sheikh* Karim al-Hassan of Harrat Salma,' she pointed out. 'You're a prince. Your dad rules a country.'

'The title bothers you, doesn't it?'

'Not particularly.' She shrugged. 'I've met people with titles before.'

And worked for them. He already knew that. And he liked the fact that she was discreet enough not to mention any names. 'Then what bothers you, Lily?'

You do, she thought. *You do.* It wasn't his title; she was used to dealing with wealthy, famous people. It was the man. The way her body reacted to him. The way he sent her into a flat spin when he so much as smiled at her. 'Nothing,' she fibbed.

'So. As I said. I'm your new apprentice.'

'You're nothing of the sort. Without a food hygiene certificate, you can't work with food.'

'I can still run errands. Make you coffee. Wash up.' He smiled, showing perfect white teeth. Sexy teeth. Sexy mouth.

Oh, Lord. She was near to hyperventilating, remembering what that mouth had done to her. Thinking about what she wanted it to do to her.

'I could make you lunch,' he suggested.

She aimed for cool. Since when would a sheikh do his own cooking? 'You're telling me you can actually cook?' she drawled.

He laughed. 'Making a sandwich isn't exactly cooking. But if you want to know just how well I can cook, have dinner with me—and I'll cook for you.'

Lord, he was confident. Most people just wouldn't attempt to cook for a professional chef, worrying that their food wouldn't come up to standard.

But she had a feeling that Karim al-Hassan would be good at everything he chose to do.

He was definitely good at kissing.

Flustered, she tried to push the memories out of her head, the insidious thoughts about what Karim might do next after he kissed her again—because he wasn't going to kiss her again. She was absolutely resolved about that. 'It's very kind of you to offer, but I'm afraid I don't have time.'

'It's Tuesday. You're not cooking tonight,' he pointed out.

'I still have preparation work to do. And my column to write. And admin—catering is the same as any other business, with bills that need paying and books that need balancing and planning that needs to be done for future events.'

'All right. Next Monday night, then. I'll cook for you.'

This was sounding suspiciously like a date. Something she didn't do.

'Or we can make it lunch, if it'd make you feel safer,' he added.

'I'm not afraid of you.' Which was true. She was afraid of *herself.* Of her reaction to him. She'd never felt like this before. This overwhelming blend of desire and need and urgency. Not even with Jeff—and she'd lost her head over him.

She'd lost a hell of a lot more, too. Her business, her home, her self-respect, and her heart. She'd worked hard to get them all back, and she knew better than to repeat her mistakes.

'So you'll have lunch with me on Monday.' It was a statement, not a question.

The sensible side of her wanted to say no.

But the woman who'd been kissed wanted to know…This

man would be a perfectionist. Would he cook as well as he kissed? Would he make love as well as he cooked?

But just as she was preparing a polite but firm refusal, her mouth seemed to work of its own accord. 'Lunch would be fine. Thank you.'

'Good. And in the meantime I'll be your apprentice. Starting now.'

'Thank you, but I really don't need an apprentice.'

'You don't have to pay me, if that's what you're worrying about. I'm giving my time freely.'

She felt her eyes narrow. 'If you're trying to get me to change my mind about catering for your business meetings…'

He spread his hands. 'I'm not trying to buy you, Lily. And time is more precious than money. If I give up my time to help you, then maybe you might reconsider giving up some of your time to help me.'

So he wanted a quid pro quo.

At least he'd been honest about it.

And he wasn't expecting to push his way into a queue. He wanted some of her non-catering days. He recognised that her time was important and he was offering her something that he valued more than money, too.

Even though she knew her head needed examining—the man was a definite danger to her peace of mind—she took a step back from the door. 'Come in.'

Karim smiled, and let her lead him to her kitchen. 'So, boss. First off, how do you take your coffee?'

'Milk, no sugar, please. And I'm not your boss.'

'I can take orders.'

He was teasing her. No way would this man take orders. Give them, yes.

She must have spoken aloud because he laughed. '*Habibti*, I can definitely take orders. Just tell me what you want me to do.'

She knew he wasn't talking about coffee or anything of the kind. There was a sensual gleam in those amber, wolfish eyes that suggested something completely different. That doing her bidding would be his pleasure—and most definitely hers.

'Coffee,' she said, before she did or said something to disgrace herself. Like telling him to carry her upstairs and rip all her clothes off and make love to her until she didn't know what day it was any more.

Coward, his eyes said. She knew he knew damn well what had just gone through her mind.

'Lots of milk or just a dash?' he asked.

'Somewhere in the middle.'

'OK. Carry on with whatever you were doing, and I'll make coffee.'

She sat at the little island in the centre of her kitchen, where she'd set up her laptop earlier that morning. So much for editing her article on summer food. How could she possibly concentrate with this man in the room? She was aware of every movement he made, even when she wasn't looking at him.

She typed and erased the same three words a dozen times.

This wasn't going to work. It was going to drive her crazy, him being in here. Invading her space. Looking in her cupboards for china—she bit back the words before she told him that she kept the mugs in the cupboard above the kettle, because she didn't want him knowing that she was watching him instead of working.

She forced herself to concentrate on the screen of her laptop.

A few moments later he brought a mug of coffee over to her—along with a plate, with a little gold box sitting on it.

Her heart missed a beat.

Then she shook herself mentally. *Stupid.* Even if he was a sheikh and impossibly wealthy, of course he wasn't going to lavish jewellery on her. They barely knew each other.

Besides, she recognised the embossing on the box: the name of a very exclusive and extremely expensive chocolatier.

'Is this what I think it is?' she asked.

'That rather depends on what you think it is.'

'Unless you've recycled the box, this is definitely chocolate.'

Again, his eyes glittered with amusement, as if he'd guessed the crazy idea she'd had a few seconds before. 'It's a new box,' he confirmed. 'I wasn't sure if you preferred white, milk or dark.'

She opened the box. He'd bought two of each sort. Enough to be a thoughtful gesture, but not so much that she felt too uncomfortable to accept his gift. From what she'd read about him online, he could've afforded to buy the contents of the shop with his spare change, and still had enough left over to buy the entire stock of the florist's next door—but he'd been restrained rather than over the top. He'd remembered what she'd said to him about not being bought.

And she liked that.

'As long as it's chocolate, I like it,' she said. 'But, as there are two of each, I think you should share them with me.'

'Thank you. I accept.' His tongue moistened his lower lip briefly. 'I have to confess to a weakness for chocolate. But I like mine dark. Rich. Spicy.'

How could the man make her think of sex when he was talking about chocolate? *Breathe*, Lily reminded herself.

He sat on the pale wooden bar stool next to hers—not close enough to crowd her, but near enough for her to be incredibly aware of his body. The first time she'd seen him, he'd worn a dinner jacket. The last time, he'd worn an expensively cut business suit. Today, he was in jeans, very soft denim that just screamed out to be touched, and a collarless white cotton shirt. It made him look younger. Approachable. And incredibly sexy.

No. Sexy was bad.

He was just…

She gave up trying to describe him, because her mind filled the gap with all sorts of descriptions that made her heart skip a beat. Hot. Touchable. Kissable.

This couldn't be happening. Shouldn't be happening. They moved in different worlds. No way could anything happen between them.

Except maybe a fling, her libido reminded her. A hot and very satisfying fling. Something temporary. No strings, no promises to be broken.

And the idea sent her temperature up another notch.

Lily reached out to take a chocolate from the box, to distract herself, and her fingers brushed against his. She found her lips parting automatically, inviting a kiss, and felt her cheeks flame when she realised that she was staring at his mouth. When she lifted her gaze she saw that he was staring at her mouth, too.

Remembering.

Wanting.

All she had to do was move towards him and she knew he'd touch her, his fingertips skating across her face and then sliding behind her neck to urge her closer. And then his mouth would touch hers. So lightly. Asking. Promising.

And this time they were on their own. There was no risk of being disturbed. No reason why he couldn't scoop her off the chair and carry her up the stairs to her bed.

She really, really had to get a grip.

She edged her chair slightly away from his. His expression told her that he'd noticed. And that he'd guessed why.

'So what are you doing?' he asked.

Trying to resist temptation, she thought. 'Editing my article about seasonal foods. Gooseberries, courgettes and broad beans.'

'It's spring now. You're talking about summer foods.'

'Magazines work three or four months in advance,' she explained. 'So although for my catering work I prefer to buy seasonal ingredients, produced as locally as possible, for this kind of work I can't.'

'So you do the pictures as well?'

'No, the magazine sends a photographer over. I've emailed them some rough shots so the designer has some idea of what the finished product looks like and can brief the photographer with the kind of angles she wants taken, and we'll be setting up the final shoot tomorrow.'

'So what are you cooking?'

'Broad beans with pancetta, gooseberry and elderflower fool, and courgette and chocolate cake.'

He looked surprised. '*Courgette* and chocolate cake? Are you sure?'

She smiled. 'Did you taste the courgettes in it yesterday?'

'That was courgette and chocolate cake?'

'Yup.'

He spread his hands. 'What can I say, other than that you're a culinary genius, Lily Finch?'

She gave him a tiny bow, acknowledging the compliment. 'We didn't tell the kids, either. Until they'd scoffed it.'

'Kids?' he queried.

Ah. She hadn't intended to tell him that. 'Never mind.'

'Talk to me, Lily,' he said softly. 'Kids?'

She flushed. 'My friend Hannah, who works with me—she takes my trials to her daughter's nursery school. Depending on what it is, they either use it for the children's break-time snacks or offer it to parents in return for a donation to nursery funds.'

'That's good of you.'

She shook her head. 'This might be a nice middle-class area now, but there are still quite a few kids around here who have nothing. Nursery's the only place where they get to play with toys and books. So this is my way of giving something back.' That, and offering a romantic dinner for two cooked by Elizabeth Finch at the nursery's annual fund-raising raffle. Because she owed Hannah for supporting her through the mess of her divorce—and she never forgot her debts.

'It's still a nice thing to do.'

She wriggled on her seat, not comfortable talking about it; he clearly noticed, because he moved over to the window and changed the subject. 'Nice garden.'

'I like it,' Lily said. 'Though it's not just flowers. There's a raised bed at the bottom which I use for vegetables, and there are pots of herbs on the patio.' She joined him at the window. 'And there at the bottom is my Californian lilac. My favourite shrub—it's a mass of bright blue flowers in May, and it attracts all the butterflies.' She shook herself. 'But this isn't getting any work done.'

'Tell me what you want me to do, and I'll do it.'

'I can't think of anything.' Well, she could—but none of those things were on the agenda. At all. She raked a hand through her hair. 'I just need to finish editing my article, and make sure I have all the ingredients in so I can make at least four sets of everything tomorrow—one finished article, two showing the cooking process at different stages, and a spare in case there's a last-minute hitch.'

'Give me your recipes, and I'll check the ingredients for you,' he said.

'Thanks, but I'd rather do it myself.'

'You don't trust me?'

'I'd rather do it myself,' she repeated. 'I can see at a glance if I need anything. It's quicker than explaining.'

'You're not a team player, then.'

Not since Jeff's betrayal. She'd vowed that she'd never, ever have another business partner again. It had been devastating to lose the restaurant she'd worked so hard to build. Even though it meant that Amazing Tastes couldn't expand, it also meant that she couldn't lose the business she loved because of someone else's failings. Been there, done that, worn the T-shirt to shreds. 'I don't have a problem with my colleagues in the kitchen.'

'But you have a problem with me?'

She nodded. 'You're…distracting.'

'Which wasn't my intention.' He smiled. 'OK. Hint taken. I'll leave you in peace. Don't worry, I'll see myself out.'

'Thank you. And for the chocolates,' she added belatedly.

'Pleasure.' He gave her a warm, sweet smile that instantly made her feel all gooey inside, then left her kitchen—which suddenly felt cooler and more shadowy. Which was ridiculous and self-indulgent, she told herself crossly.

'I'll see you in the morning,' he called—and then closed the front door behind him before she could protest that, no, he couldn't possibly turn up tomorrow, because she was busy and...

'Argh!' Lily suddenly realised she'd pressed the wrong button and accidentally deleted her entire article. She said something very pithy, then stalked over to the kettle to make herself another cup of coffee and calm down before tackling her laptop's 'recycle bin' and making it give her article back.

Karim al-Hassan had a lot to answer for. He was distracting, irritating...and impossibly sexy. And even if she sent him away when he turned up on her doorstep tomorrow morning, she wouldn't be able to get him out of her head.

Where was her professionalism when she needed it?

'Just be sensible. You know what happened last time,' she told herself.

But Karim wasn't Jeff, an insidious voice said in her head. Karim was a man who believed in honour. The attraction was very much mutual. There was no reason why they couldn't act on that attraction. Keep it between themselves. Provided he wasn't actually seen out with her, the chances were that the paparazzi would leave them alone. And adding him to her client list would be the perfect cover...

Ha. There was an old saying that if something appeared too good to be true, it usually was.

And, as she had no intention of picking herself up, dusting herself down, starting all over again and struggling to get back to where she was right now, she'd have to think of a way to get Karim out of her head and out of her life.

CHAPTER FOUR

LILY was pretty sure that she was ready to face Karim, the next morning. That all her arguments were marshalled neatly and they were completely persuasive.

Then she discovered that she wasn't ready at all.

Far from it.

Because when she opened the door to him, he disarmed her with the sweetest of smiles and a large terracotta pot full of violets.

'They're dog violets. Although they don't have a scent like sweet violets, apparently they attract butterflies.' His eyes crinkled at the corners. 'I would've liked to give you a proper bouquet—roses, lilies and what have you—but I don't want you thinking I'm trying to buy you.'

So instead he'd given her something much less showy, the kind of floral gift that appealed to her much more. Clearly he'd been listening to what she'd said, the previous day, about liking flowers that attracted butterflies. The dog violets would be perfect for her patio. 'Thank you. They're lovely.' So pretty: a soft lavender blue with a white throat. And he'd taken time out of his day to find these for her—she knew without having to ask that he hadn't just sent an assistant to pick up the first thing she saw in a florist's. 'Where did you find them?'

'In a little shop down the road from my place. They'll go well with your thyme, even though these are both cultivated.'

'Violets and thyme?' Thyme was pretty, but it was a savoury herb, and these weren't the sort of violets she'd crystallise and use to decorate a cake. What was he talking about?

Obviously her confusion showed, because he said softly, 'I know a bank whereon the wild thyme blows, Where oxlips and the nodding violet grows.'

'Poetry.' Though not something she recognised.

'Shakespeare. *A Midsummer Night's Dream.*'

Clearly he'd expected her to know the quote. 'Sorry.' She shrugged. 'I've never really been into the theatre.'

'You like films?'

'Yes, but I don't get the time to go to the cinema. I don't really watch TV, either,' she admitted.

'So what do you do for relaxation?'

She damped down the pictures in her head, of tangled white sheets and Karim's skin sliding against her own. 'I cook,' she said simply.

'It's more than just a job to you, isn't it? It's your passion.'

'It's my life,' she said. And she hoped he understood that she meant it.

He closed the door behind him; she thought at first he'd followed her to the kitchen, but then she realised he'd stopped before the watercolour in the hallway, her favourite, one of lavender fields in Provence.

'That's a beautiful painting.' He looked at the signature, then at her. 'Amy Finch. Is she any relation?'

'She's my mother.'

He joined her in the kitchen. 'Were you ever tempted to follow in her footsteps?'

'No. It was always cooking, for me. Though I suppose some of it's rubbed off, because presentation's an important part of cooking—you need to make it look nice when you plate it up.' Memories brought a lump to her throat and a wave of home-sickness—which was crazy, because she was still in England.

Amy was the one who'd moved abroad. 'On rainy days in school holidays or at weekends, Mum would get her huge old cookery book off the shelf, open it at random and then close her eyes and circle her finger over the pages—wherever her finger landed, we'd cook that recipe. Or we'd improvise if we didn't have all the ingredients in the cupboard.'

'You're close to your mum?'

'I don't see her as often as I'd like, but we speak a lot. She lives in France now—in Provence. That picture's the view from her house, the lavender fields.' She unlocked the conservatory doors and placed the pot on the patio, near to the terracotta pots full of lavender from the fields her mother had painted, then closed the doors again and washed her hands.

Karim glanced over at her oven. 'You're already cooking something?'

'That's the finished article,' she said. 'I'm cooking it now because it needs time to cool before Hayley does her stuff.'

'Hayley being the photographer?' he queried.

She nodded.

'So what time is she going to be here?'

'Midday.' Lily took a deep breath. Time to tackle him about this apprentice thing, make him see how crazy and unworkable it was. 'Look, Karim, I know you mean well, but—'

'I won't get in your way,' he interrupted softly. 'Humour me. I'll fetch and carry whatever you want. I'll even wash up for you without complaining.'

'Wash up?' She couldn't help smiling at the thought. 'You're telling me I'm going to have a prince washing up in my kitchen?'

'If you're being picky, it's sheikh rather than prince.'

'Same difference.'

He leaned against the worktop and looked at her. 'I'm a perfectly ordinary person, you know.'

There's nothing ordinary about you, Lily thought—and then really, really hoped she hadn't said that aloud.

'Besides,' he continued, 'if you're afraid of getting your hands dirty, you'll be no good as a leader. You need to see what has to be done and make sure it gets done. If you can't delegate a task because there simply isn't time, then you have to do it yourself.' He rolled his eyes. 'What, do you think I have an enormous staff or something?'

'Don't you?'

'No. I admit, I use a laundry service because life's much too short to iron shirts.'

'Agreed.' She used a laundry service for her chef's whites, but everything else went through her washing machine and then was hung to dry on hangers to minimise creasing and avoid ironing. 'And I bet you have a cleaner.'

He spread his hands. 'I admit, someone comes in a couple of hours a day.'

'And cooks for you, too?'

'No. I do that myself. And, before you start accusing me of being princely for having a cleaner, just about any other business-man living on his own would do the same thing. Time spent cleaning the house is time you can spend more profitably at work.'

'Bottom line,' Lily stated, 'you have staff.'

'They're not live-in.' He paused. 'Except my assistant—whose duties include security.'

She felt her eyes widen. 'You have a bodyguard?'

'Just one and, as I said, he's also my assistant. He's not scary. Provided you're not threatening me, that is,' Karim added meditatively. 'Then, I guess, he might be.'

'But…you're here on your own. You were on your own at Felicity's party.'

'Rafiq is discreet.'

Colour scorched into her cheeks. 'You mean, he was on the balcony that night?'

'No.'

'But he knew.'

'He knew that I was talking to you on the balcony, yes.'

She'd just bet that Karim's bodyguard had guessed exactly what his boss had really been doing. Some of the newspaper articles she'd seen had talked about the playboy desert prince. 'And he knows you're here now.'

Karim walked over to her and pressed his fingertip lightly against her mouth. Just as he had, that evening, before he'd kissed her. For one insane moment, Lily actually considered opening her mouth and taking his finger lightly between her teeth.

Bad, bad idea, she remonstrated with herself. Hayley would be here in a couple of hours—and a couple of hours wasn't nearly long enough to do what she wanted to do with Karim al-Hassan.

Which was completely crazy. She took a step backwards.

'You don't have to be afraid,' Karim said softly.

Oh, but she did. Not of him. Of *herself*.

'It's standard procedure.'

'In your world. Not mine.'

For a moment, his eyes were shadowed. And then he nodded. 'Rafiq's been with me for a long, long time. I trust him with my life—literally.'

'So where is he now?'

'Outside. Doing his job.'

'So, what, he's going to frisk Hayley at the door when she arrives?'

'That's a bit over-dramatic.' Karim frowned. 'I thought you said you didn't watch much television?'

'I don't, or I would've thought about this before. You're royalty, so of *course* you're going to have a bodyguard. And if he's stuck waiting outside while you're slumming it in here, the poor man's going to be bored out of his skull. Tell him to come in.' And apart from basic hospitality, it would mean that she and Karim weren't on their own. An added safety net.

'Firstly, I'm not slumming it, as you so delightfully put it. Secondly, he won't be frisking Hayley. And, thirdly, I could tell him to come in, but he'd refuse.'

Lily blinked. 'Is he *allowed* to refuse your requests?'

Karim laughed. 'You mean, I snap my fingers and everyone jumps to my orders?'

'Yes.'

He spread his hands. 'You haven't.'

'That's different. I'm not from your country and I'm not one of your staff.'

'Actually, I prefer people who work with me to think for themselves. They have a job and they know what needs to be done. I trust them to do it without having to give them step-by-step instructions. Rafiq does the job his way.'

'But—' The timer on the oven pinged, interrupting what she was going to say. She switched it off, checked that the cake was done, then put the tin to cool for a few minutes on a rack.

Karim watched her deal efficiently with the cake. Despite the fact that she was wearing a very unfeminine and traditional chef's outfit—a thick white cotton jacket teamed with baggy black-and-white chequered pants—she still managed to look all curves. Desirable. He wanted to mould his palm over the curve of her buttocks. And he wanted to do a lot more than that. He wanted to unbutton the jacket and slide it off her shoulders. What would she be wearing underneath? A camisole top? Or a lace-trimmed bra? Or—

He'd better stop thinking about that before he embarrassed them both. 'As you're in chef's clothing, I'd expect you to wear a hat.'

'You mean a traditional toque, with a pleat in it for every single way I can cook an egg?'

It was his turn to blink in surprise. 'A pleat for every single way you can cook an egg?'

'Uh-huh. Which in practical terms means up to a hundred. The more pleats, the better the chef.'

'There are a hundred ways of cooking eggs?'

She laughed. 'Trust me, there are. But, no, I don't wear a toque. They're not that comfortable, especially because it means I have to pin my hair up. My Buff deals with it much better because it encloses my hair.'

'Buff.' He knew the word in a different context. A much more pleasurable one.

'It's tubular so I can tuck my hair in it—and when I fasten it my hair stays fastened too,' she explained. 'It's microfibre cloth, so it's cool when the kitchen's boiling. Much more practical than the old-fashioned chef's hat. Which, by the way, very few people wear nowadays.' She shrugged. 'If I had short hair, I'd probably use a skull cap.' She glanced at the clock. 'Right. I need to start getting things ready.'

'I'll start with the washing up,' Karim said.

She shook her head. 'You'll start by making that poor man a drink. I assume you know how he takes his coffee? Or would he prefer tea?'

Karim smiled. 'We've been here for long enough for him to like English coffee.'

'Then you know what to do.'

So she was taking the same approach that he did—telling him what needed to be done and just letting him get on with it? Karim hid his amusement and made the coffee. He took a mug out to Rafiq—who, predictably, said that he was staying put—and then returned to find Lily working her way through a list, ticking things off. Although she wouldn't let him touch the food, citing his lack of a hygiene certificate, she let him get dishes out for her. And the more he watched her work, the more impressed he was. She seemed to do six things at once, but when he looked closely he realised that she was managing her time brilliantly, performing every task in the right order and switching from one to another at the most effective point. A critical path analyst could learn a lot from just watching her for a morning.

And, even more impressively, he discovered that she could do all that and hold a conversation at the same time.

'So are you permanently based in England?' she asked.

'I have been for the last five years, but I'll be going back to Harrat Salma in a few months' time,' he said. 'I might take on some of my father's duties, or I might take an ambassadorial role and travel a bit. That's still under discussion.'

'But on the whole your future's pretty much mapped out?'

'Pretty much,' he admitted. 'Eventually I'll take over from my father, and obviously then, although there will be some travelling involved, I'll be based in Harrat Salma.' And there was another duty he'd have to perform. Producing an heir to the throne. 'And I imagine my parents will start marriage negotiations once I'm back home permanently.'

'Marriage negotiations?' She blinked. 'You mean, you're not even going to be able to choose your own wife? That's outrageous!'

'Far from it. Look how many so-called marriages for love end in divorce.'

She flushed. 'It's not always like that.'

'The statistics aren't on the side of love. What is it, practically two in three marriages ending in divorce? People talk about love, but it's nothing of the kind. It's a relationship based on lust and infatuation. And when that dies, the marriage dies with it because there's nothing left to support it.'

'That's incredibly cynical.'

'It's incredibly accurate,' he corrected. 'The statistics bear it out.'

She shook her head.

He shrugged. 'It worked for my parents. They respect each other and there's a deep affection between them.'

'Isn't that the same thing as love—respect and affection?' Lily asked.

'Maybe. Maybe not. Affection is something that grows with time.' He spread his hands. 'My parents didn't lose their heads and rush into an unbreakable contract with someone unsuitable. That's not what marriage is all about.'

'So what is it about?'

'It's about having similar expectations, working together towards the same end. It's about trust and respect and honour.'

'I can't believe you're actually going to marry someone you don't know.'

He rolled his eyes. 'It's not as if I'll only meet her on the morning of the wedding.'

'And what about physical attraction? Or are you going to have a harem to deal with—?' She stopped abruptly, looking embarrassed.

'Having sex?' he finished, guessing exactly what had been on her mind. The same as his. Going to bed with each other. 'Now you're talking fairy tales. We practise monogamy. And I would always be faithful to my wife. I'd never insult her by taking a mistress.'

'I'm not maligning your honour.' She blew out a breath. 'I just can't believe that you're talking so dispassionately about this—as if marriage is a business arrangement. Especially when the papers say you date a different woman every week.'

'Firstly,' he said, 'marriage is a business arrangement. And secondly, I date a lot, but it doesn't necessarily mean I sleep with all my girlfriends. And besides, they know the score—that I'm out for mutual enjoyment but I'm not able to promise them anything permanent. It's my duty to marry and produce an heir to my country, and I trust my parents to choose someone who will suit me and suit Harrat Salma. Yes, I will have some say in it, but I have to put my country first.'

'That's so cold-blooded.'

'It's sensible,' he corrected. 'Divorce is out of the question. I have a duty to my country. So I need to marry the right person—someone who will support me, someone I can trust and respect. The affection will grow between us afterwards.'

'But what if you fall in love with someone?'

'That's not going to happen.' He smiled wryly. 'I'm twenty-eight, *habibti*. If I were going to fall in love with someone un-suitable, I would've done it already.'

She still couldn't quite get her head round this. How he could be so cool and calm and discuss his future marriage as if it were a business arrangement.

Then again, she'd married for love. She'd been head over heels when she'd walked down the aisle to Jeff. And look what a disaster that had been.

She busied herself with ingredients, chopping and mixing and making sure he couldn't see her face. Couldn't see her struggling with the temptation to break all her rules—a temp-tation that was growing second by second.

Knowing that he would have to go through an arranged marriage, Karim wasn't free to have a permanent relationship with someone. And he was going back to his country in a few months' time. Which meant that having a fling with him would be safe—she could act on that incredible attraction between them. By definition, their relationship would have limits; it would have to end as soon as he left England. And because she knew that right from the start, her heart wouldn't get involved.

And maybe, just maybe, after the last four years of working hard and the months of utter misery before that, she deserved some fun.

A fling.

Mutual pleasure.

At half past eleven, Lily stopped. 'Is Rafiq a vegetarian?' she asked.

'No,' Karim said.

'Is there anything he can't eat on religious or health grounds?'

'No.'

'Good.' She busied herself chopping salad; then she slit a couple of pitta breads open and deftly filled them with sliced chicken and salad. 'Take him some lunch—and when the shoot's over he's very welcome to pudding.'

He was impressed that she'd thought of it. 'Thanks.'

'And it's up to you if you want to have lunch now, or eat what I make, after the shoot. The broad beans and pancetta work just as well cold as a salad as they do hot as an accompaniment.'

'Whatever's easiest,' Karim said. 'You're not going to eat until afterwards, are you?'

'No.'

'I'll join you, then.'

Just after he'd returned from sending lunch to Rafiq, the photographer arrived. Lily seemed completely at ease with the older woman, so he guessed they'd worked together quite a few times before.

'Hayley, Karim—Karim, Hayley.' Lily introduced them with the minimum of fuss.

For a moment, he wondered if Hayley would recognise his face. Though if she worked for the lifestyle magazines rather than the glossy gossip pages, she probably wouldn't.

'So how do you know our Lily?' Hayley asked.

'Through a mutual friend.'

'Ah.' There was a wealth of supposition in that tiny syllable. Clearly Lily didn't normally have 'friends' in her kitchen during the monthly photo-shoots—which set him apart from other people.

She looked at him with a professional eye, then walked over to the window. 'Hmm. You'd look good in one of these shots. On Lily's patio, eating that gooseberry fool.' She grinned. 'You'd have all the women sighing over you.'

Karim shook his head. 'Thanks, but no.'

Hayley nodded knowingly. 'I see. Pity.'

'What's a pity?' Lily asked.

'That all the best-looking men are gay,' Hayley said ruefully.

She definitely didn't recognise him, then. And Karim was highly amused that Hayley had misread him so badly. He was unable to resist asking, 'And what makes you think I'm not Lily's lover?'

Hayley burst out laughing. 'No offence, love, but our Lily isn't known for dating. She's married to her kitchen.'

Interesting. *Very* interesting.

'So if you're here,' she continued, 'you really are just a friend. And, looking the way you do, with nice manners and being dressed so beautifully…'

'I see,' Karim said, mirroring her earlier tone.

His eyes said something different to Lily—that he wasn't her lover…*yet*.

'All right. I'll do the shoot.'

'You don't have to,' Lily said, sounding almost panicky.

'Relax, *habibti*. It's fine.' He winked at her. 'Just let me know where and how you want me to sit, Hayley,' he said.

'Excellent. We'll do the inside shots first,' she said.

Hayley might be blunt—and completely wrong about the situation between him and Lily—but she was a good photographer, Karim thought. Her directions were clear and concise. She brought out the best in Lily as well as in the food. And watching Lily as she cooked…it was beautiful. Almost as if her movements were choreographed.

When Hayley was satisfied with the indoor shots and Lily had poured the gooseberry fool into a dozen pretty glass bowls, Hayley set up her tripod outside. She directed Karim where to sit and adjusted his pose several times.

It was Lily's turn to watch the photography session. And Hayley was absolutely right, Lily thought. Dressed in another of those collarless white shirts and stone-coloured chinos, Karim looked the epitome of summer. He was perfect for the shot.

And the way he licked the gooseberry fool off the spoon, under Hayley's direction, would make any woman seeing the magazine feel hot and bothered. He was making Lily feel distinctly hot and bothered.

He gave her a sultry look, and she felt her nipples tighten in response.

Oh, Lord.

She was just glad that her chef's jacket was so thick that it hid her body's reaction from him. And she really, really hoped that her thoughts didn't show in her face.

When Hayley had gone—taking a large chunk of the chocolate cake wrapped in greaseproof paper with her—Lily sent Karim out to Rafiq with the gooseberry fool, hoping that she'd be able to get her libido under control before he came back.

Fat chance.

She needed half an hour under a cold shower for that to happen.

When he walked back into the kitchen, even though her back was turned she knew the second he set foot in the room. Her libido sat up and started begging.

'Hey. This is my job. You've done all the hard work.' He took the dishcloth from her, and nudged her aside from the sink with his hip.

Even though the contact between their bodies was casual, and there were several layers of clothes separating them, it was all too easy to imagine his skin sliding against hers. His body pushing into hers. Her body closing round his.

'Lily? Are you all right?'

'Uh.' She swallowed hard, trying to drag her mind back out of the gutter. 'Thanks for your help today.'

'My pleasure.'

'And, look—Hayley pretty much pushed you into those shots. If you'd rather not have a photo of you in the magazine

I'll have a word with my editor, explain the situation and ask her not to include it.'

'It's not a problem, Lily.'

'But you're...' She grimaced. 'Isn't it kind of like giving royal approval to my recipes?'

'Fine by me.' He shrugged. 'I approve of that gooseberry fool. Very much.'

That wasn't what she'd meant, and she knew he was deliberately avoiding the issue. 'Won't it cause a problem for you back in Harrat Salma?'

'No. Hayley merely took a shot of your friend sitting on your patio, enjoying a summery pudding.' He continued washing up. 'Who I am has nothing to do with it.'

'But people are going to recognise you.'

'So what if they do?'

'I...' Defeated, she gave up. If it didn't bother him, why should it bother her?

He smiled at her. 'I enjoyed it, actually. It was a lot of fun.'

'Hayley said she thought you were used to having your photograph taken.'

He shrugged. 'I am.'

'But she thought it was because you were a model or something.' She felt her skin heat. 'And she was convinced you were gay.'

His grin broadened. 'If only she knew that the whole time I was licking that spoon, I was imagining tasting *you.*'

Oh, damn. The picture that put in her head. 'Karim.' She breathed his name.

The teasing light disappeared from his eyes, replaced with something much more intense. 'It's going to happen, Lily,' he said softly. 'Sooner or later, it's going to happen. Between you and me.'

Even though she'd been thinking about it earlier, that had been the fantasy. This was the reality. And suddenly she panicked. 'I don't...'

'Date? So Hayley said.' He moistened his lower lip. 'Sometimes rules are made to be broken.'

The last time she'd broken a rule, she'd ended up with a broken heart. Not to mention a broken business. And enormous debts. Even though she knew the situation with Karim was different, the old fears swamped her into silence. She wanted him. Really wanted him. And despite her earlier thoughts about not letting herself get involved, she was scared that she might end up being in too deep.

As if he guessed how much she was panicking, he dried his hands, then took her right hand. Drew it to his lips. 'It'll be OK,' he said softly. 'More than OK. You just need to trust me.'

Trust.

Now, there was a sticking point.

She wasn't sure she was capable of trust any more. 'I...' Frustrated that she couldn't find the right words to explain it—not without telling him just how naïve and foolishly trusting she'd once been—she shook her head.

'Lily, I'm not going to hurt you.' He was still holding her hand; he turned it over, dropped a kiss into the centre of her palm and folded her fingers over it. 'I think right now you need a breathing space, so I'm going to leave now. But you know where I am if you want me.'

If she wanted him?

Of course she wanted him.

But this was all way too complicated.

'Later, *habibti*,' he said softly. 'Later.'

CHAPTER FIVE

LILY slept badly that night. Every time she closed her eyes, she could see that intense look in Karim's eyes. Could hear him saying, 'The whole time I was licking that spoon, I was imagining tasting *you*.' Could feel the warmth of his mouth against her skin…and it drove her crazy, making her ache with wanting.

When the alarm finally dragged her out of a fitful sleep, her head felt like lead and there was a dull ache across her brow. A cup of coffee, two paracetamol and washing her hair in a cool shower made the headache go away, but they did nothing to stop the unnatural heat in her veins. Nothing to stop the anticipatory kick in her stomach at the thought of seeing Karim.

For a moment, she considered going out to buy her supplies before Karim arrived, so she wouldn't be there to answer the door to him—but that would be the coward's way out. And Elizabeth Finch wasn't a coward.

'Good morning,' Karim said when she opened the door to him dead on nine o'clock.

'Good morning. You know where the kettle is, so feel free to make yourself a coffee.'

He glanced at her feet. 'You're wearing shoes.'

'I need to go to the market this morning. The earlier, the better.'

'Which market?'

'The street market round the corner,' she explained. 'There are a couple of organic veg stalls. If I go now I'll get the best choice for my client.'

'Of course. You're catering tonight.'

She nodded. 'I need to go to the butcher's, too.'

'Fine. But, first…' He handed her a bag. 'Better to leave this here than take up space in your basket. Plus it's a bit fragile, even with the bubble-wrap around it.'

'What is it?' she asked.

'You'll see when we get back. Do you have your bag? Your list? Your keys?'

She blinked. 'We're going to the market right now?'

'That's what you said you wanted to do,' he reminded her. 'So let's go.'

'You're going with me?'

He raised an eyebrow. 'As your assistant…yes. I'll carry your shopping for you. Though I'm flattered that you trust me enough to leave me alone in your house.'

So he was still playing that game. She sighed. 'Karim, it'd be easier if you didn't go with me. For goodness' sake, you're His Royal Highness Prince Karim al-Hassan of Harrat Salma.'

'A title doesn't stop me carrying your shopping.'

'What if the paparazzi find out and follow us?'

'Actually, they don't tend to bother with me much, except at parties,' he said with a smile, 'because I'm incredibly boring.'

Boring? Karim? Ha. As if she were going to fall for that one.

'Don't worry. You're not going to find your picture splashed all over the tabloids, along with a few paragraphs of speculation about how long you've been sleeping with me.'

She felt her face heat. 'You haven't slept with me.'

'So I haven't.' And even though he didn't say it, she could see the word in those amazing amber eyes again: *yet*.

She knew it was a promise.

Desire rippled down her spine, and she looked away, not

wanting him to see just how tempted she was. It would be, oh, so easy to reach out, pull his head down to hers, and kiss him the same way he'd kissed her on Felicity Browne's balcony. She could still remember how it had felt when he'd kissed her palm yesterday, the warm, erotic pressure of his mouth against her skin, how much she'd wanted him to follow that through— touching his lips to the pulse-point in her wrist and then tracing a path up to the inner curve of her elbow, her shoulder, the sensitive spot at the side of her throat, her collarbones.

To her relief, he misconstrued the reason why she'd turned away and put the bag on her hallway table. 'You won't have photographers camped outside your door or anything like that,' he reassured her. 'You're safe with me. And it'll be nice not to have to carry everything home yourself, will it not?'

Carry. She wished he hadn't said that word. Because she could imagine him carrying her. Upstairs. To her bed.

She made a non-committal noise, not daring to speak in case the wrong words burst out. She was going to get these crazy feelings back under control. She *was*.

'Lily?'

Against her better judgement, she said, 'OK. If you really want to, you can come to the market with me. But you can't play at being my apprentice today. I'm cooking, and there are such things as health and safety regulations. I don't breach them. Ever,' she added, just so he was clear that she always played by the rules in business.

'I would expect nothing less of you,' he said softly. 'How about tasting?'

Finally, she nodded. 'Provided you use clean cutlery, and you use it only once, tasting's fine.'

'Tasting's fine? Good. I'm glad you said that. Because I really need to…' To her shock, he dipped his head and brushed his mouth against hers in a kiss that was completely chaste and yet incredibly sensual at the same time. It was over almost as soon as it had begun—and left Lily wanting so much more, her hands were actually shaking as she grabbed her handbag and shopping basket, then locked the front door behind them.

Karim didn't say a word as they walked together down the street. But every so often, the back of his hand brushed against hers. Casually. Accidentally.

On purpose?

But his expression was inscrutable. She had no idea if he was doing it deliberately or not. But every touch sensitised her skin; her nipples tightened and excitement coiled low in her belly.

No wonder he had a reputation as a playboy.

She'd never met anyone as sensual as Karim al-Hassan. And she'd certainly never thought that a simple visit to the market would bring her to fever pitch. She managed to force herself to concentrate, make sure she didn't miss anything off her list, but by the time they got back to her house she was a wreck. And even though she tried pretending she was cool, calm and sophisticated, she wasn't in the slightest. He knew it, too, because she fumbled her keys and dropped them.

'Allow me, *habibti*.' He retrieved them and unlocked the door, holding it open for her before scooping up the basket and following her indoors.

Lord, she needed a cold shower. Ice cold, so the temperature shocked her brain back to where it should be instead of being lost in erotic fantasies about Karim al-Hassan.

But a shower wouldn't be practical right now.

Particularly as she didn't trust herself not to invite him to join her.

She needed caffeine. 'Coffee,' she mumbled.

'I'll make it.'

Funny how he was already at home in her kitchen. Knew where everything was, moved around without having to search for things or ask her. And he looked right there, too.

Don't start getting any crazy ideas, she warned herself. There couldn't be any future between them. Apart from the fact that she had no intention of letting a relationship derail her life again, he'd already told her that he would return to his desert kingdom, marry someone chosen by his family, and raise the next generation of heirs. If—*when*—something happened between them, it would only be a fling. It couldn't be more than that.

Get a grip, she told herself mentally, and busied herself putting things away. By the time she'd finished, Karim had made coffee for them and taken a mug out to Rafiq. And when he returned, he brought the paper bag she'd left on her hallway table.

'For you, *habibti*,' he said.

She took out the bubble-wrapped parcel, carefully unwrapped it, and stared in surprise. It looked like an intricate carving in the shape of a rose. 'Thank you. It's beautiful. Is it a carving from Harrat Salma?'

'It's not a carving—it's a desert rose,' he explained. 'Gypsum, with sand inclusions; in arid, sandy conditions the mineral crystallises in a rosette formation. Hence "desert rose".'

'It's lovely, but I can't accept something this valuable.'

He smiled. 'It's a mineral, *habibti*, not a diamond. You simply dig these up in the desert.'

'You dug it up yourself?' Then, before he could answer, she held up a hand to stop him. 'Of course you did. You said yesterday, a good leader's not afraid to get his hands dirty.'

'Precisely.'

There was a wistful look in his eyes, but it was there for such a short space of time that she wondered if she'd imagined it; within moments he was back to being his usual urbane, charming self, asking her about the finer points of planning a menu for a balance of texture, colour and taste. And she knew he wasn't questioning her judgement: he was trying to understand what she did, how she worked.

He spent the rest of the morning with her, and then he

reached out to take her hand. 'I'm distracting you, *habibti*. This apprentice thing isn't going to work, is it?'

'No,' she admitted.

'Pity.' He rubbed the pad of his thumb over the back of her hand. 'You're distracting me, too, you know. You should see the pile of paperwork in my office.'

She bit her lip. 'So what are you suggesting? That we call it a day?'

'Not quite. Because, *habibti*, the last few days have shown me how good you are at time management. I think you have capacity to expand a little.'

'In other words, you still think I can manage to fit in the catering for your presentations.'

'Exactly. So I'm going to give you some space to think about it. Decide what you want to do.'

Lord, he was persistent, but at least he was giving her a choice. Perhaps she could give up some time on her freer days, fit in the flexible elements of her work where she could, and do what he wanted. It meant she'd be crazily busy for those weeks. She'd lose all her thinking time.

But with Karim around, she'd lost her thinking time anyway. She'd found herself being distracted by his presence all week, by fantasies of what she wanted him to do with her.

'Tell me your answer on Monday,' he said.

'Monday?'

'When you're having lunch with me,' he reminded her. 'I'll send a car.'

'I'm perfectly capable of get—' she began.

'I know you're perfectly capable of organising your own transport,' he cut in. 'Just humour me, this once. Rafiq will collect you at half past eleven on Monday.'

'Half past eleven,' she repeated.

'Good.' He was still holding her hand; he raised it towards his mouth, but instead of giving her a polite kiss on the back of her hand he turned her wrist over. Touched his mouth to the point where her pulse was beating madly.

Her knees went weak.

He couldn't stop there.

Please, don't let him stop there.

All thoughts of him being off limits went completely out of her mind. The only thing she was aware of was Karim. The sound of his breathing. The exotic scent of his aftershave. The way her skin had heated up under his mouth.

And she wanted him to continue. Desperately wanted him to continue.

As if he could read her mind, he pushed up the three-quarter-length sleeve of her T-shirt and teased her inner elbow with tiny, nibbling kisses that made her practically hyperventilate.

'Karim.'

'I know,' he said quietly, straightening up and looking her in the eye. His pupils had expanded, leaving a tiny rim of bright golden iris around them. 'It's the same for me. My head's telling me not to do this while my body's saying something completely different. And watching you cook, the way you move…It's been driving me insane.'

'I can't stop thinking about the balcony. About when you kissed me. And I want…' She shivered.

'Ah, Lily.' He dropped her hand and cupped her face in both hands. His mouth brushed against hers, so very lightly—and yet it felt as if she'd been scorched.

The next thing she knew, her hands were fisted in his hair and his arms were wrapped tightly round her, and his mouth was jammed over hers. Somehow he'd moved so that he was sitting on one of the bar stools; he'd pulled her onto his lap so that she was straddling him.

Two layers of soft denim between them.

Too many layers of denim between them.

His erection pressed against her and she couldn't help rocking slightly, shifting closer.

He tore his mouth away from hers. 'Lily, you blow me away.'

It was very much mutual. She couldn't see straight, couldn't think straight. And she wanted his mouth back on hers, right now. She caught his lower lip between her teeth, nipping just hard enough to make him open his mouth—and then she kissed him the way he'd kissed her. Sliding her tongue into his mouth, exploring and tasting and inciting him, the way he'd incited her. Hot and wet and wanting.

The pressure against her clitoris intensified as he moved slightly, rocked against her. She moaned into his mouth, wanting more.

And then, just as suddenly as he'd started, he stopped.

'My self-control's hanging by the tiniest, thinnest thread,' he said. 'Part of me wants to say to hell with health and safety—I want to rip off your clothes and mine, and take you right here, right now, on this granite worktop.' He paused. 'But.'

She shivered. Such a tiny word, yet it felt so huge. 'But?'

He dragged in a breath. 'But I don't have a condom. And I'm pretty sure you don't, either.'

'No,' she admitted. 'I…' Her voice tailed off. How stupid and unsophisticated he must think her. She couldn't even remember the last time she'd dated anyone, let alone the last time she'd made love.

'It's OK.' This time, his kiss wasn't consuming. It was gentle, soothing, telling her that everything was fine. 'This isn't exactly normal for me, either.'

'No?' She didn't believe a word of it. Karim was six feet two of pure masculinity, exotic good looks combined with those intense amber eyes. Even without the added inducements of his title and his wealth, women would fall at his feet if he clicked his fingers. And hadn't the newspapers called him the playboy prince?

'No. I date, sure.' He drew the pad of his thumb along her lower lip. 'But I don't get distracted. I don't skip work with the flimsiest of excuses, just to spend time with someone.'

'You skipped work for me?'

'I rearranged my schedule,' he said. 'Worked late to make up for it.'

He'd rearranged his schedule to spend time with her. The thought warmed her. 'So what are we going to do…about this?'

'I know what I want to do,' he said huskily. 'But I'm not going to be selfish about this. You have a business to run. And although we both know I could make you forget all about it—just as you could make me forget what I'm doing—that wouldn't be fair. To either of us. So I'm going to do the noble thing.'

'Which is?'

Gently, he shifted her off his lap. 'I'm going to leave you in peace. Give you time to think about it—to think about what you want to do.' He stole another kiss. 'To think about what you want me to do.'

Just as well she was holding onto the worktop. Because the thoughts that put in her mind made her knees weak.

'And we'll talk on Monday.'

Monday.

Four whole days away.

Four days to get her sanity back: or four days to drive her demented and utterly desperate for him. Right at that moment, she had no idea which way it was going to go.

'Monday,' she said.

'Later, *habibti*,' he said. He brushed his mouth against hers just once—light, teasing, enough to make her mouth tingle and her body beg for more.

And then he was gone.

CHAPTER SIX

FOUR days of breathing space.

And every single second of it dragged.

Lily found herself missing Karim. Really missing him. And, although she made sure she gave her clients the service they were used to from her, she knew her heart wasn't completely in her work. She'd always been so excited by cooking, loved what she did. But now…everything felt faded, dull, in comparison with him.

'Want to talk about it?' Hannah asked on the Saturday night.

'About what?'

'Whatever's been distracting you for the last few days.'

More like whoever, Lily thought. 'I'm fine,' she fibbed.

'Hmm. I worry about you, Lily.' Hannah hugged her swiftly. 'You work too hard and, since Jeff, you've never…' She shook her head. 'Sorry. That wasn't tactful. And considering my marriage ended up in a mess, too, I don't blame you for not wanting to get involved with anyone. But it's been four years for you, Lily. I think it'd do you good to go and have some fun.'

'Have a fling, you mean?'

The words were out before she could stop them.

And Hannah's look of surprise turned quickly into interest. 'You've met someone?'

'Yes. No. It's complicated.' Lily wrinkled her nose. 'Well. It's sort of complicated. There couldn't be any future in it.'

'I would ask if he's married,' Hannah said, 'but I know you'd never do that.'

Lily appreciated her friend's belief in her. 'No, he's not married. But he's…' How could she explain without telling Hannah the full details? 'He's not going to be around for long.'

'So it'd be like a holiday romance?' Hannah spread her hands. 'That sounds perfect to me. No ties, no involvements, so you don't have to worry that he's going to let you down. You can just have fun, enjoy it while it lasts and move on afterwards.'

Put like that, it sounded like the perfect solution. 'Is it really that simple?'

'Of course it is.' Hannah smiled at her. 'Go for it. It'll do you good.'

They were too busy for the rest of the evening to discuss it further, but even though Lily was rushed off her feet she still found herself clock-watching. It grew even worse when she was at home during the day. The minutes seemed to stretch into hours. Several times, she picked up the phone and started to dial Karim's number before cutting the connection. It wouldn't be fair to distract him; he had work to catch up on, too. Besides, he was the one who'd suggested four days of breathing space.

Four days to decide what to do.

Cook for him? Or sleep with him?

Could she be greedy and do both?

Was it possible to have it all?

Cooking for Karim would be a challenge. She had a feeling that he wouldn't want sandwiches and savouries for his business meetings, and this could be a chance to explore a completely different cuisine. Broaden her repertoire. And although it would mean that her schedule was crazy and she'd be shattered by the end of it, it would only be temporary. She could move the more flexible side of her work around, lose some of her free time.

Besides, she liked what she'd seen of Karim. She wanted to help him.

And if she was going to break one of her rules, she might as well break all of them.

Temporarily.

By Monday morning, she was convinced that all her blood had turned to adrenalin. She couldn't settle to anything. And she was shocked to realise that she was more flustered by a simple invitation to lunch than she had been by any important rush-job at work.

For a start, she had no idea what to wear.

This was lunch, not an actual date, so she could keep it casual. Jeans and a T-shirt. Then again, it was going to be a business discussion. Maybe the black dress she wore to clients' houses…But no. Last time she'd worn that outfit, Karim had kissed her stupid and she'd wanted him to remove every scrap of her clothing.

She still wanted him to do that.

But she needed to get the business side of it sorted first.

In the end, she chose tailored black trousers, a slate-blue camisole top, and a black lacy shrug. With high heels, she looked businesslike rather than casual. Particularly because she took care over her make up. And she pinned her hair up in a chignon rather than pulling it back at the nape of her neck, the way she usually did at work, or leaving it loose.

She had enough time to spend an hour at her laptop—pretending to plan her column for the next month and trying very hard not to think about the fact she was going to break all her rules and make love with Karim this afternoon.

Then Rafiq arrived to collect her.

'Miss Finch? This way, please.'

'Thank you, Rafiq.'

It felt odd, sitting in the back of the enormous black car. She was more used to driving herself, in the small van she used for work, or taking the Tube. Rafiq was polite but not particularly chatty, and when she tried to ask him about Karim he clammed up even more. Karim could definitely rely on his assistant-cum-bodyguard's discretion.

And then at last Rafiq pulled into a parking place. He came round to open Lily's door for her, then escorted her to the foyer of an expensive-looking block of modern flats.

'You're not coming with me?' she queried.

He spread his hands. 'Karim gave me the afternoon off. Though he knows where I am, should he need me.'

Rafiq was close enough to his employer to use his given name rather than something more formal, Lily thought; he'd certainly been formal with her. Though it hadn't been a disapproving sort of formality. He'd actually smiled as he'd thanked her for her kindness in sending out lunch and coffee for him on the mornings when Karim had been playing at being her apprentice.

'Well, have a nice afternoon, Rafiq.'

He regarded her with almost a smile. 'And you, Miss Finch.' He gave a small bow. 'You need to press the top buzzer,' he said, gesturing to the intercom.

So Karim had the penthouse flat, did he? That didn't surprise her. She pressured the buzzer.

After a short pause, Karim answered. 'Good afternoon, Lily.'

'Good afternoon.'

'I'm on the third floor. Take the lift.'

She did so, relieved that the lift wasn't the kind with mirrored walls. She didn't want to see whether she looked as nervous as she felt.

There were two doors in the corridor. One was obviously a fire door, which led to the stairs; the other was Karim's front door. And in between was what seemed like acres of deep-pile carpet. She took a deep breath, walked steadily over to his front door, and knocked.

A few moments later, he opened the door. Smiled at her. And the look in his eyes made a pulse throb between her legs. 'Hello, Lily. Come in.' He ushered her into the flat.

The carpet there, too, was deep enough for her to sink into it. She slipped off her shoes, not wanting to ruin his carpet, and the soft wool caressed her insteps as she followed him into his living room. The room was enormous, light and airy, with what looked like a balcony or a terrace outside the floor-to-ceiling window. The walls were painted a deep sand colour, and rich silk hangings in jewelled tones were placed to catch the light. The sofas were low and overstuffed, upholstered with what looked like expensively soft leather—the sort you could sink into and never want to get up from. There was a sculpture on a low table, and photograph frames on the marble mantelpiece that looked as if they were enamelled but she suspected were works of art in themselves, studded with gems.

Even though she was used to being in the homes of the rich and famous, his flat was something else. Understated, tasteful—and very, very expensive. A completely different world from her own. Yet another reminder of the gulf between them.

But those sexy amber eyes were regarding her in a way that made her nipples tighten and her temperature rise a notch. And she'd spent the weekend arguing with herself: this was going to be safe. A fling with limits. She wasn't going to get hurt. Everything was going to be just fine.

'What would you like to drink?' he asked.

'Something soft, please.'

'Sure. Come through.'

His kitchen was almost as large as hers, incredibly tidy and full of the kind of equipment she'd been tempted by but that had been outside her budget. Instead of an island, there was a granite-topped table in the middle.

The words echoed in her head. *I want to rip off your clothes and mine, and take you right here, right now, on this granite…*

Oh, Lord.

Faced with this incredible kitchen, she didn't know whether she wanted to explore, start cooking, or just rip off Karim's clothes and straddle him on the kitchen floor.

'Lily?'

She shook herself. 'Sorry. Staring. Lusting.' To her horror, the last word slid out before she could stop it.

He laughed. 'Over my kitchen? Or—' his voice dropped an octave, grew husky with promise '—over me?'

Over him. Definitely over him.

Flustered, she took a box from her handbag and gave it to him. 'I meant to give you these. To say thank you for lunch.' The same kind of expensive chocolates that he'd bought her, the previous week. And she'd remembered what he'd told her: he liked his chocolate rich and dark and spicy.

He looked at the box and smiled his approval. 'I love these. Thank you. They'll go well with the *gahwa saada*—traditional Arabic coffee—at the end of our meal,' he said.

Something smelled gorgeous: she recognised the scent of spices and garlic and tomatoes. And he'd talked about Arabic coffee. 'You've made me a traditional meal from your homeland?' she guessed.

'You questioned whether I could cook. So I thought I'd show you rather than tell you. I put most of it together last night, so the flavours had time to infuse and mature.'

'But…as a prince, don't you have servants?'

'In Harrat Salma, yes. Here, no. Anyway, we've had this conversation. I cook for myself. I enjoy it—it relaxes me. Gives me time to think.' He shrugged. 'Arabic cooking involves time. Patience.' His eyes held hers. 'A virtue that's always rewarded.'

She had a feeling she knew exactly what kind of reward he had in mind.

The same one that she did.

This was impossible.

But he'd said something else, something that had surprised her. About letting flavours infuse. 'You think like I do about food.' She frowned. 'So why do you need me to cook for you? Why can't you just do it yourself?'

'Because, *habibti*, although I'm perfectly capable of multi-tasking, I can't cook in my kitchen and hold a business meeting in a different room at the same time. Nice idea but, as you pointed out to me last week, the laws of physics rather get in the way.' He took a jug from the fridge and filled two heavy-based plain crystal tumblers. 'Anyway. *Ya hala.* Welcome to my home.'

'Thank you.' She took a sip. 'This is very refreshing.'

'It's traditional orange *sharbat*. And what's in it?' he tested.

'Freshly squeezed orange juice and sparkling water—and you've clearly steeped mint in it for a while.'

'Not bad. But there's one ingredient left.'

She shook her head. 'Tell me.'

'Orange-blossom water.' He took a bottle from the fridge and handed it to her.

She couldn't resist taking a sniff. 'This'd be lovely in a sorbet, and to flavour some crisp biscuits to accompany it.'

'Nice idea. I'll remember that.' He looked at her. 'So. Are you ready for lunch, *habibti*?'

'Thank you. Is there anything I can do to help?'

'It's all done. Come and sit down.' He led her through to the dining room. The dining table was huge, more like a boardroom table, and in one corner of the room there was a glass-topped desk where she guessed he worked, but all the office equipment was hidden away behind frosted glass.

The table stood in front of the huge floor-to-ceiling windows with a view over the park; a blue damask runner was centred on the pale wood, set with granite placemats, silver cutlery, white porcelain and more of the plain crystal glasses. Again, there were rich abstract hangings on the walls, though this time they were in marine shades, toning with the dark blue curtains and pale blue walls.

'It's a beautiful setting,' she said.

'What were you expecting—a low table, silk cushions and a tented ceiling?' he teased.

'Maybe not the tented ceiling, exactly—but, given the scent in the kitchen…yes, I was expecting the rest,' she admitted.

He spread his hands. 'It can be arranged. As the saying goes, all I need to do is snap my fingers.'

'Very funny. Next you'll be telling me that you have a genie.'

'Djinn,' he corrected. 'No.' He glanced meditatively upwards. 'A tented ceiling wouldn't be right here, because I couldn't go outside and see the desert stars.'

'You can't see any stars in London,' she said, understanding exactly what he meant. 'It's one of the things I love about going to see Mum and Yves in France—I can sit outside and watch the stars.'

'Your mother and brother, they don't live in a city?'

'My mother and stepfather.' Of sorts, but it was too complicated to explain. 'They live in Provence. In the middle of nowhere. Well, they're about thirty minutes from the airport in Marseille, and there's a town about ten miles away, so they're not completely cut off from civilisation—but it's far enough away that there's practically no traffic around the vineyard or the village. Life's slow, and you can just relax and unwind in the sun.'

'Like in the desert,' he mused. 'But I'd bet serious money that the stars in Harrat Salma are like nothing you've ever seen.'

'You miss it, don't you?'

'Yes and no. I've been based in England for over half my life,' he said.

'So you went to school here?' she asked.

'When I was thirteen,' he said.

'It must have been hard, leaving your family.'

'I wasn't completely on my own. My b—' He stopped abruptly and his face grew shuttered. 'Anyway. Time for lunch. Sit down, *habibti.*'

What had he been about to say? His brother? And yet she couldn't remember seeing any reference to a younger or older brother in the news stories she'd glanced through. Just stunning models and actresses, with lots of blonde hair and incredibly long legs.

He brought in several platters, then took a seat opposite her.

'You've gone to a lot of trouble. Thank you.'

He shrugged. 'As I said, I enjoy cooking. It helps me think. Now, may I help you?' He talked her through the dishes; circassian chicken, tabbouleh and felafel she knew, but not the *hashweh,* courgettes and aubergines stuffed with a mixture of lamb, rice and spices, and the *shakshouka,* peppers stewed with garlic, tomatoes and coriander.

'Fabulous,' she said when she'd tasted each in turn. 'You know, you're really brave, cooking for me. Most people panic at the thought of cooking for a trained chef.'

'I don't panic easily.' He spread his hands. 'And I'd rather hear your professional opinion rather than your polite guest's opinion.'

She looked at him. 'There's a good balance of tastes and textures. You've got bread to mop up the juices, which is good—couscous or rice wouldn't work, as you already have grains in the tabbouleh. The only thing I'd ask is, I assume it's meant to be served warm rather than hot?'

He inclined his head. 'We're doing this the traditional way. Though I suppose in a way it's like Mediterranean food—the Greeks, too, serve their food warm rather than hot.'

'If you ever decide you don't want to be a sheikh any more,' she said with a smile, 'just go on a course and get yourself a food hygiene certificate.'

'And be your apprentice again?' he asked.

'No. Cooking as well as this, you'd make partner in a week,' she said.

'Partner.' His eyes glittered. 'I'll bear that in mind, *habibti*.'

She knew he was talking about a different type of partner. Not a business partner—a lover.

And she also knew that she was going to accept his offer. Maybe even instigate it.

Her mouth went dry, and her hand was trembling very slightly as she lifted the glass of orange juice to her mouth.

Pudding was a rosewater-scented sorbet, sprinkled with pomegranate seeds.

'Now that's a good combination,' Lily said. 'Taste, texture and colour.' She pressed one of the pomegranate seeds to the roof of her mouth, feeling the flavour burst over her tongue. 'Oh-h-h. Luscious.'

'Pomegranates represent forbidden desire,' Karim said.

'Persephone.' A story she remembered her mother telling her, a story connected with a painting at an exhibition Amy had taken her to see as a special treat.

'Some cultures believe that Eve was tempted with the pomegranate rather than an apple,' Karim said.

Temptation.

A word she could definitely associate with Karim.

She could imagine Karim feeding her a pomegranate, seed by seed, as she lay with her head on his lap, and the thought made her temperature go up a notch. Because the picture in her head grew clearer, sharper. Of Karim bending down to lick a stray trickle of juice from her lips. Of his mouth against hers, hot and demanding. Of…

'*Habibti*?' he asked. 'Are you all right?'

No. She wanted him. Here. Now.

It was an effort to get herself back under control. 'I'm fine,' she fibbed.

He allowed her to help him clear the table, but refused to let her wash up. 'And now I'm going to make you coffee.'

He gestured to one of the bar stools; she sat down and watched as he took a pot with a long handle, measured water in a tiny handle-less cup and poured it into the pot, then added two teaspoons of coffee.

'So you make Arabic coffee like Turkish coffee,' she said, fascinated.

'Sort of, but we add other things—some people add saffron and some add orange blossom water, but I tend to do it the traditional way. One teaspoon of coffee per cup and half a teaspoon of spice.'

She watched as he added a teaspoonful of crushed cardamom, heated the coffee, then removed the pot from the heat until the foam started to subside. He poured a small amount of coffee into two small handle-less cups made of white china, with a wide band at the top in an intricate silver pattern.

'Welcome to my house, Lily. To your health.' He handed the cup to her.

'Thank you. And to yours,' she responded. She tasted the coffee as he watched.

'Do you like it?' he asked.

'I think it's an acquired taste,' she said diplomatically.

He gave her a mischievous smile. 'You're meant to drink three cups, to be polite. It's very rude to refuse.'

'Three whole cups?' She could maybe manage one. But three?

'Not full cups. That's why we only put a little in, each time. Three little sips,' he said. 'The first is for health, the second is for love, and the third is for future generations.' He poured her a second mouthful. 'You wobble your cup very slightly from side to side when you've had enough. Like this.' He demonstrated.

'But it's rude to refuse.'

He inclined his head. 'However, we're in your country, not mine. I'm hardly going to send you to the tower and have you clapped in chains for refusing any more coffee.'

'I'm glad to hear it.' The first for health. The second for love...

She took another sip. 'Karim. The last four days have been—' She broke off, not wanting to admit just how much he affected her.

'I know,' he said softly. 'For me, too. I nearly cracked at three o'clock yesterday morning. Except I didn't think you'd appreciate a phone call right at that moment.'

'I was probably awake,' she admitted. Thinking of him.

'So you've had time to think about the situation.'

She nodded. 'This is driving me crazy. Driving us *both* crazy.'

'I know. I can't get you out of my head. Every time I close my eyes, you're there. And I never let myself get distracted like this.'

'It's the same for me,' she admitted wryly. 'It's a seriously bad idea. Completely against my better judgement.'

'Agreed.'

She could see that he was looking at her mouth. Just as she was looking at his. Wanting. Needing.

'Let's do this,' she said in a rush. 'Let's get it out of our systems.'

'Are you sure?'

She wasn't sure that it'd get him out of her system. But she was sure that if she didn't give in to her body's urging, she'd go insane.

He was clearly waiting for an answer. So Lily wobbled her cup, the way he'd shown her. Put it down on the worktop. Then she walked over to him, slid her hands into his hair, and drew his mouth down to hers.

CHAPTER SEVEN

THE first touch of Lily's mouth on his broke Karim's self-control. And then he was kissing her back, his arms wrapped tightly round her. He could feel the softness of her breasts against his ribcage, the warmth of her skin through her thin camisole top and his shirt, and it wasn't enough. He wanted more. So much more.

That camisole top was driving him crazy. With the lacy shrug, her shoulders were covered, and the neckline wasn't plunging. She looked perfectly modest. And yet, at the same time, the material clung to her curves, as close to her skin as he wanted to be.

And she'd kissed him first.

He loved the fact that she'd been brave and honest enough to tell him what she wanted. Even more than that, he loved the fact they wanted the same thing. This was completely mutual. They'd both been holding back—and now they didn't have to, any more. They could give in to this crazy, whirling desire.

And he knew it was going to be amazing.

Still kissing her, he slipped the lace shrug from her shoulders and placed it behind him on the kitchen worktop. And then he broke the kiss so he could trace a path with his lips down her throat, across to her shoulder. He hooked one finger under the spaghetti strap of her top and the clear strap of her bra, drawing them both down to bare her shoulder. Taking his time, he kissed his way along the skin he'd just bared, breathing in her scent.

She tipped her head back, offering him her throat. He took full advantage, kissing the curve of her throat and lingering in the hollows of her collarbones before drawing the straps down to bare her other shoulder.

He nuzzled his way along her skin, breathing in her scent as he kissed her. 'You smell of…mmm…dulce de leche.'

'It's my shower gel.'

'It's gorgeous.' He dragged in a breath. 'Though I'm afraid it makes me want to taste you, Lily. Touch you. Make love with you.'

'Then do it,' she said, her voice husky and sexy as hell. And her pupils were enormous, so huge that her eyes looked almost black. It looked as though she wanted this—needed this—as much as he did.

'Sure?' he checked.

'Absolutely sure.'

'Good.' He slid one arm round her, then bent to scoop his other arm under her knees, lifting her up. She held onto his shoulders for balance, and he couldn't resist stealing another kiss before carrying her into the hall and up the stairs.

'Karim? I thought this was a flat?'

'It is. It's on two floors,' he said. 'Downstairs is the living quarters and my office. Upstairs is for sleep and bathing.' And, oh, he was looking forward to sharing a bath with her. Lathering her skin. Sluicing the foam off her again. And touching her until she was quivering and begging him to enter her.

He nudged his bedroom door open with his foot and carried her over to the bed before setting her on her feet again, letting her slide all the way down his body.

'If you're going to change your mind, Lily, do it now,' he said. 'Because once we pass the point of no return…' It was a promise rather than a threat. Once they passed the point of no return, they were going to paradise. Both of them.

She looked him straight in the eye, proud and unafraid. 'I'm not going to change my mind.'

'Good.' He cupped her face in both hands. Dipped his head. Brushed his mouth so lightly against hers in the sweetest, gentlest kiss. Then he pulled back just far enough to look into her eyes. Serious grey-blue eyes. Eyes that told him just how much she wanted him.

'Hold that thought,' he whispered, and went over to the window to close the curtains. He left the blinds where they were, so enough of the bright spring sunshine filtered into the room to let him see her.

She was still standing where he'd set her down; he walked back over to her and took her hand again. Held her gaze. Kissed the tip of each finger, drawing it briefly into his mouth until he could see the flare of desire brighten in her eyes. And then he took the hem of her camisole top and drew it upwards. She lifted her arms, letting him pull off her top; although he'd intended to fold it neatly and put it over the back of the chair, his brain forgot to send the message to his fingers and he ended up simply dropping the garment on the floor. He traced along the lacy edges of her bra with one fingertip, enjoying the contrast between the stiffness of the black lace trim and the softness of her pale, pale skin. 'Lily. You're so beautiful,' he breathed.

'Thank you.' Her cheeks bloomed with colour.

He was charmed by her blush. She didn't take compliments for granted, and he liked that.

'This is, um, a tad uneven.' She gestured to her state of undress and then to the fact that he was fully clothed.

'Do something about it, then,' he invited.

She held his gaze for a long, long moment, and then she began to unbutton his shirt. Precisely, carefully. She pushed the material off his shoulders; he had no idea where it landed and he didn't care, because then Lily was touching him. She stroked his arms, his shoulders, then let her hands trail down over his chest to his abdomen. 'Karim al-Hassan, you're beautiful, too.' Her fingers brushed against his abdomen again, and his body tightened. 'I take it you're a regular at the gym, to get a six-pack like this?'

'Not as much as I should do,' he admitted. 'Especially as my best friend owns several health clubs and nags me about the importance of exercise. But I play squash a couple of times a week, and I eat reasonably sensibly.'

She licked her lower lip; unable to help himself, he bent his head and caught her lip between his, sliding his hands down her sides and moulding them to her curves.

He wanted that chignon out of the way, too. He didn't want her smooth and sophisticated and businesslike. He wanted the passionate woman beneath, all tumbled hair and sexy pout. He searched for the pins in her hair, found them and gently removed them.

'Gorgeous. So soft,' he said softly as her hair fell over her shoulders. This was how he remembered her on the balcony, her mouth full from kissing and her hair mussed and her eyes full of desire.

He reached behind her back with one hand and unclipped her bra; then sucked in a breath as the garment fell and her breasts spilled into his hands. The perfect fit. Her nipples were all rosy and hard and just begging for him to touch them.

So he did. He dipped his head and took one nipple into his mouth, teasing it with the tip of his tongue and then sucking hard.

She dragged in a breath. 'Karim.'

He stopped immediately, hearing the quiver in her voice. 'Too much?'

She shook her head. 'No. I want more. A lot more. I want everything you can give me.'

'Greedy.' He nipped gently at her skin. 'Guess what?'

'What?'

'I'm greedy, too. I want everything you can give me, too, Lily. I want you so badly, it feels as if I'm burning up.'

She rested her hand briefly against his forehead. 'You are. Probably because you're still wearing too much and you need to strip off.'

'So what do you suggest we do about it, *habibti*?'

She gave him the wickedest smile he'd ever seen, then undid the button of his chinos and let her hand rest against the zip.

For a moment, he couldn't breathe, he wanted her so much. He wanted to feel her hand curled round his shaft. Wanted to feel her stroke him, tease him, wrap her legs round him. Wanted to fit himself to her entrance and slide into her hot, tight wetness.

Maybe he said the words aloud—he had no idea. He couldn't think straight any more. But then she slowly undid his zip. Pushed his chinos over his hips. Curled her fingers round his erection through the soft jersey of his jockey shorts, all the while keeping eye contact and giving him that wicked, wicked smile. And he found himself almost hyperventilating.

'Lily. Keep this up and I'll last all of five seconds,' he warned, when he was able to speak.

She trailed one finger along the length of his erection, still with that barrier of soft jersey between their skin. And now it was her turn to tease him, licking her lower lip and looking all the way down his body and all the way up again. 'So what do you suggest, Karim?'

Talking was off the agenda. Definitely off the agenda. He needed to act. Right now.

He undid the button of her trousers, slid the zip down, and gently pushed the soft material over her hips. And then she was standing before him in nothing but a tiny pair of black lace knickers and bright pink nail polish on her toes.

The ultimate temptation.

And right now she was all his—just as he was all hers.

Nothing else mattered.

He ripped off the rest of his clothes, shoved his duvet aside, scooped her up and laid her on the bed.

Lily couldn't remember desiring anyone so much—even Jeff, in the days before he'd hurt and disillusioned her. Karim was just perfect. He wasn't lean and skinny, but he wasn't fat either: just beautifully toned, with powerful shoulders and strong biceps and narrow hips and strong thighs. He really did look like a desert prince. And the contrast between his olive skin and her own very fair English complexion made her shiver with pleasure.

His hands were sure yet gentle as he tipped her back against the pillows, and when he kissed his way down her body, his face was soft and smooth against her skin. Obviously he'd shaved that morning.

And somehow he'd found erogenous zones she hadn't even known existed, making her wriggle beneath him, desperate for more. He circled her navel with his tongue, nuzzled her hip bones, and finally, finally removed her knickers and slid his hands between her thighs, parting them; but when they moved lower, caressing the backs of her knees, she almost whimpered.

She knew now exactly how he'd felt when she'd teased him through his underpants. Hot. Desperate. Wanting all the barriers gone so they could be skin to skin. So he'd be inside her.

'Karim. Stop teasing me. Please. I need…'

'I know, *habibti*. So do I,' he whispered, and kissed her swiftly before climbing off the bed.

Despite being completely naked, he was totally unselfconscious; Lily couldn't help watching him as he moved. He really was beautiful. Perfect musculature beneath that smooth olive skin. And she *wanted*.

He rummaged in his chinos, took out his wallet and removed a condom.

'My job, I think,' she said, taking it from him as he joined her on the bed again. She undid the foil packet, then slid the condom over his erect penis; and she was gratified when he gave a sharp intake of breath.

He knelt between her thighs, and she sank back against the pillows—purest, softest down. Karim stole another kiss, then whispered, 'Lily?'

She opened her eyes. 'Yes?'

'Now?'

'Now,' she confirmed.

Slowly, gently, he eased his body into hers. Slow, measured thrusts, going a little deeper each time, letting her body get used to his size and his weight.

And it was driving her crazy.

Lily had had sex before. Made love before. But nothing had prepared her for this. This strange feeling of…completion. That after a long, long journey, she'd finally come home.

This really shouldn't be happening.

She knew that she and Karim had no future together. How could they, when he was royal-born and would eventually go home to rule his desert kingdom with his family's chosen bride by his side?

And besides, she'd promised herself that this would be temporary. That her heart wouldn't get involved.

'This feels like paradise,' Karim said softly.

He slid his hands up her thighs, gently positioning her so that her legs were wrapped round his waist, and then he pushed deeper. Lily couldn't help giving a little 'oh' of pleasure. Karim smiled, but not as if he were smugly pleased with himself; more that he was pleased he was making her feel so good.

He kissed her throat—hot, wet, open-mouthed kisses that had her quivering and clutching at his shoulders, wanting him even closer, needing the ultimate contact. She was aware of the hardness of his chest against the softness of her breasts, and the friction of the hair against her sensitised nipples made her shiver—too much and not enough, all at the same time.

And then, as if Karim knew she was right near the edge, he slowed everything down. Slowly, so incredibly focused, he withdrew until he was almost out of her, then slid all the way back in again, putting pressure on just the right spot and making her feel as if she were floating. She should've guessed that he'd be as good at making love as he was at kissing—at cooking— at practically anything he put his mind to doing. But then he adjusted his rhythm to suit hers, stoking her desire higher and higher until she couldn't think about anything else except the way he made her feel.

When her climax hit, it was amazing: as if she were in a ballroom somewhere, dancing cheek to cheek with him, with the light of a thousand candles reflecting off a mirror ball in the centre of the room and whirling round her, making her dizzy.

'Now,' he whispered, and jammed his mouth against hers; she felt his body surge against hers, and knew that he too had just fallen over the edge.

It was a while before Lily floated back to earth. She found herself curled up against Karim, her head resting on his shoulder and her arm wrapped round his waist; his hand was resting on the curve of her hip. She felt warm and comfortable and safe, and it would be, oh, so easy to let herself drift into sleep—and let him wake her later with kisses and caresses.

Considering that it was a Monday afternoon, this was incredibly decadent. Lazing in bed together, as if they both didn't have other things to do.

'So what's the verdict?' she asked softly. 'Got it out of your system?'

Karim turned on his side and shimmied slightly down the bed so he was facing her, then brushed his mouth against hers. 'Not yet. How about you?'

'Not yet.' She smiled wryly. If anything, it had made the wanting worse. Because now she knew what it felt like to make love with Karim al-Hassan, she wanted to do it all over again. And again. 'So what happens now?'

He kissed the tip of her nose. 'You're all warm and soft and naked—and, best of all, in my arms. In my bed.' He nuzzled the curve of her neck. 'Mmm, and you still smell of dulce de leche. So my vote is I go and get those fabulous chocolates you bought and we stay right where we are. Unless you really, really have to be somewhere else this afternoon?'

'I don't mean now as in "right this second".' She shifted, looking awkward. 'Though it's the middle of the afternoon. We really ought to get up.'

'There's no ought,' he countered. 'But I take it you mean "now" as in "after this".' He brushed a strand of hair from her face. 'We *could* pretend this never happened.'

He might be able to, but she knew she'd find it a struggle.

'Or,' he said thoughtfully, 'we could carry on. But, Lily, I'm not going to lie to you. I can't offer you anything permanent.'

'I know that. And I'm not looking for a relationship anyway. I don't have room in my life.' She smiled wryly. 'Having sex with you—I just broke my personal rules. And I'm going to break the rest of them, too. I was going to tell you earlier, except...' She shivered. 'You distracted me.' And how. 'Anyway. I'll cook for you.'

'Business and pleasure don't mix.' He shook his head. 'Forget about the business meetings, Lily.'

'But they're important to you, aren't they?'

'I'll manage.'

He hadn't answered the question, so she knew the answer. They were important.

'You don't have to manage.' She laced her fingers through his. 'We're talking lunch and coffee, yes?'

'Yes. Morning and mid-afternoon coffee.'

'Then it's doable. Whatever days they are. If I get Hannah to do the shopping for me, I can cook for you in the mornings. And I have a couple of people I can call on when I need extra waiting staff—if you don't mind, they'll do the afternoon coffee, but I'll have cooked everything they serve.'

'I don't want to put pressure on you.'

She laughed wryly. 'Says the man who spent the best part of last week under my feet, distracting me.'

'Because I was being selfish and not looking at things from your point of view. As you said, everyone needs time off. If you fit in catering for my meetings on top of your current bookings, you'll be working stupid hours. You won't get any time to yourself.'

'Do you take time off?' she asked.

'No,' he admitted. 'There's always someone to see, a report to read, leads to follow up, plans to make.'

'Well, then. What's sauce for the goose, as they say. Yes, it'll be crazy, but it's a short term thing—a one-off.' As their affair would be. 'So I'll manage.' She paused. 'So what is it you actually do?'

He blinked. 'I thought you looked me up on the Internet?'

'I did. Just long enough to find out that you were Prince Karim al-Hassan of Harrat Salma.' She paused. 'And a serial party-goer with a taste for tall, glamorous, posh blondes.'

'Yes, to the first.' He rolled his eyes. 'The second is pretty much spin. For the record, I'm very attracted to a certain small, curvy woman with brown hair.' He twined the ends of her hair round his finger. 'Not that your hair's plain brown. It has gold and copper strands in the sunlight. Natural highlights.'

She couldn't resist it. 'Don't split hairs.'

'You have a very bad taste in puns, *habibti*.'

She laughed. 'So your life isn't a round of lunch appointments and cocktails and parties, then?'

He sighed. 'Yes and no. It looks like it is, I admit. But parties are the quickest way to network—to meet the people who can usefully do business with me. You can't promote something without some degree of partying.'

'So who are you really? Underneath the spin?'

Karim thought about it, not sure how to answer. Although it was something he didn't usually talk about, he felt compelled to be honest with Lily. To tell her the truth. He released her hair and lay back against the pillows. 'By training, I'm a vulcanologist.'

'A vulcanologist?' She blinked. 'You're telling me you have volcanoes in your country? But…' She shook her head. 'You're from Arabia. I thought…'

'Lawrence of Arabia, endless dunes and camels? No. We have deserts, but they're not all sand. That's why my country's called Harrat—that's the Arabic name for the lava fields around a volcano,' he explained.

'And they're active?'

He smiled. 'In Harrat Salma, not for thousands of years—though there were eruptions in Yemen, one in 2007 and others in the last century, and in the Red Sea in the century before that.'

'You've studied them?'

'In situ,' he said. 'My degree was in geology.' And half a doctorate in vulcanology. But she didn't need to know about that bit. About the fact he'd had to walk away from the studies he'd loved, without a backward glance. 'I loved every second of it. Especially the field trips, back in my country. I remember one incredible field trip when we spent the night sleeping in a volcano crater. We could see the minerals sparkle round us in the moonlight; it was like sleeping among the stars.' An experience he thought adventure travellers would enjoy, too. Those holiday expeditions were the one thing he'd promised himself that he would lead.

Not that he could, now that he was the heir instead of the spare.

'A vulcanologist,' she said in wonder. 'That's the last thing I would've guessed. I mean…there aren't even any volcanoes in Britain.'

'Actually, there are,' he corrected. 'Not active ones, but Edinburgh's built on an extinct volcano—Arthur's Seat.'

'So where's the nearest active volcano to here?'

'Italy or Iceland.' He shifted so that her head was on his shoulder and her arm was round his waist, while he cradled her against his body and curled the ends of her hair round his fingers again. It had been so, so long since he'd talked about this. But he had a feeling that Lily would understand. She had a passion for what she did, too. 'I loved Iceland. Seeing the midnight sun and the ice fields—so very different from home, and yet the land is the same in places. The lava fields.'

'Hot springs and ice hotels,' she said.

'They're pretty spectacular. And the Northern Lights. Even when you know how they're formed, they're still magical. Unearthly.' He dropped a kiss on the top of her head.

She cuddled into him. 'You're the same about volcanoes as I am about cooking.'

Yes. Once. But he couldn't afford to follow his heart now. His duty was more important. 'Was,' he corrected. 'I don't have time for it any more.'

She pulled back slightly to look him in the eye. 'And you miss it.'

Yeah, he missed it. Missed it so much that he blocked it out with work and constant partying, so he didn't have time to think about his previous life. 'I'm too busy to miss it,' he said. It was true—just not the whole truth.

'I really didn't expect this. A vulcanologist,' she said again in wonder.

'So what did you expect?'

'It's obvious there's more to you than being a serial partier. I assumed you did something with oil or money,' she said.

'We're not an oil-rich country.' He looked at her. 'Why money?'

'From the way you speak, I'd say you went to a public school over here. Then you studied at Oxford or Cambridge— I would have guessed a degree in economics or business studies, maybe followed by an MBA.'

He was surprised that she could tell so much just from his voice. 'I'm impressed. Apart from the subject of my degree, you're spot on. I went to Eton and then Cambridge. And I did my MBA in London.'

'Did you enjoy it?'

'I enjoyed the intellectual challenge,' he said, using his professional voice. The one he used with journalists. The one that gave nothing away.

'But it's not like your volcanoes. It didn't touch your heart, did it?'

Was it that obvious? He made a non-committal noise, not wanting to be disloyal to his family.

'At least your parents let you follow your heart for a while.'

'Yes.' The lump in his throat stopped him telling her why he'd stopped following his heart. His parents had been perfectly happy to let him study volcanoes while he was the second son. But when his brother Tariq had died, the whole world had turned upside down. And he'd known in his heart what he had to do.

His royal duty.

How could he put his parents through having to ask him to give up the career he loved and come back to step into Tariq's shoes? It would have made things so much harder for them. So, the moment he'd put the phone down, he'd left his volcanoes behind. Forgotten about becoming Dr Karim al-Hassan and gone straight to his parents. Grieved with them. And that day he'd told them that he was coming home to Harrat Salma. That he would try to live up to Tariq's abilities.

It had been his choice.

'Don't clam up on me,' she said softly. 'Tell me.'

He couldn't.

Not yet.

'I need a shower,' he said, wanting to avoid the subject. 'Come and join me.'

She pressed a kiss into his chest. 'Karim.'

He shook his head. 'I don't want to talk about it. I'm fine.'

'Bottling things up isn't good for you,' she said softly.

'I'm fine,' he repeated. 'Come on. I want to introduce you to my shower.' Something he knew would be spectacular enough to take her mind off what he'd told her—and stop her asking questions to fill in the rest of the gaps.

'That's a shower?' she asked when he led her into his bathroom.

'It's a wet room,' he said. There were oversized tiles on the walls with a narrow cobalt-blue border running across the room, and frameless glass panels around the shower area. A granite shelf jutted from the wall under a mirror, with a clear glass bowl basin balanced on top of it and most of the plumbing hidden away—just the taps showed, in polished chrome.

'That's stunning,' she said. 'I think you've just convinced me that my old-fashioned bathroom is—well, old-fashioned.'

'But it suits your house. An old-fashioned bathroom wouldn't look right in this flat. It's modern. It's all about glass and light.' Which was the whole reason why he'd bought it.

'Don't you miss having a bath, though?'

He gave her a wicked grin. 'I have a bath, all right. I'll introduce you to it, later—it's in a different room. But this is my shower.' He took her hand and drew her within the glass panels. 'Would you like a waterfall or rain?'

She looked at him, clearly not understanding.

Oh, she was going to love this. Almost as much as he was going to love sharing this with her. 'We'll start with rain,' he said, savouring the moment, and switched on the water.

PLAY LUCKY 7 and get FREE Books!

HOW TO PLAY:

1. With a coin, carefully scratch off the silver area at the right. Then check the claim chart to see what we have for you—**2 FREE BOOKS** and **2 FREE GIFTS—ALL YOURS FOR FREE!**

2. Send back the card and you'll receive two brand-new Harlequin Presents® novels. These books have a cover price of $4.75 each for the regular-print edition or $5.25 each for the larger-print edition in the U.S. or $5.75 each for the regular-print edition or $6.25 each for the larger-print edition in Canada, but they are yours to keep absolutely free.

3. There's no catch. You're under no obligation to buy anything. We charge nothing—ZERO—for your first shipment. And you don't have to make any minimum number of purchases—not even one!

4. The fact is, thousands of readers enjoy receiving books by mail from the Harlequin Reader Service. They enjoy the convenience of home delivery and they like getting the best new novels at discount prices, **BEFORE** they're available in stores.

5. We hope that after receiving your free books you'll want to remain a subscriber. But the choice is yours—to continue or cancel, anytime at all! So why not take us up on our invitation, with no risk of any kind. You'll be glad you did!

FREE GIFTS!
We can't tell you what they are... but we're sure you'll like them!
2 FREE GIFTS
when you accept our No-Risk offer!

Visit us online at www.ReaderService.com

Scratch off the silver area with a coin. Then check below to see the gifts you get!

Slot Machine Game!

YES! I have scratched off the silver box above. Please send me the 2 free books and 2 free gifts for which I qualify. I understand I am under no obligation to purchase any books as explained on the opposite page.

❑ I prefer the regular-print edition

306 HDL EXFL   106 HDL EW69

❑ I prefer the larger-print edition

376 HDL EXFW   176 HDL EW7L

FIRST NAME

LAST NAME

ADDRESS

APT.#

CITY

HX-P-07/09

STATE/PROV.   ZIP/POSTAL CODE

7	**7**	**7**	Worth **TWO FREE BOOKS** plus **TWO FREE GIFTS!**
🍒	🍒	🍒	Worth **TWO FREE BOOKS!**
♣	♣	♣	Worth **ONE FREE BOOK!**
🔔	🔔	🍒	**TRY AGAIN!**

➤ Detach card and mail today—No Stamp Needed ➤

The Harlequin Reader Service—Here's how it works:

Accepting your 2 free books and 2 free mystery gifts (gifts valued at approximately $10.00) places you under no obligation to buy anything. You may keep the books and gifts and return the shipping statement marked "cancel". If you do not cancel, about a month later we'll send you 6 additional books and bill you just $4.05 each for the regular-print edition or $4.55 each for the larger-print edition in the U.S. or $4.74 each for the regular-print edition or $5.24 each for the larger-print edition in Canada. That is a savings of at least 15% off the cover price. It's quite a bargain! Shipping and handling is just 25¢ per book.* You may cancel at any time, but if you choose to continue, every month we'll send you 6 more books, which you may either purchase at the discount price or return to us and cancel your subscription.

*Terms and prices subject to change without notice. Prices do not include applicable taxes. Sales tax applicable in N.Y. Canadian residents will be charged applicable provincial taxes and GST. Offer not valid in Quebec. Credit or debit balances in a customer's account(s) may be offset by any other outstanding balance owed by or to the customer. Please allow 4 to 6 weeks for delivery. Offer available while quantities last.

CHAPTER EIGHT

'OH. MY. God.' Lily had seen this kind of bathroom fitting in the 'dream house' kind of magazines Hannah loved—but this was the first time she'd been up close and personal to one.

The shower head was square, and the area of the spray was large enough to cover them both completely. And when the water flowed down, it really was like being in a rainstorm in the middle of summer. She closed her eyes and lifted her face up to the spray, loving the feel of it against her face.

Karim took the shower gel from an alcove in the wall and lathered her thoroughly. He paid attention to her shoulders and her back, working the knots out of her muscles, then slid his hands down to the curve of her waist, letting them drift lower, to her buttocks.

And then he turned her round to face him. 'Good?'

'Very good.' She was almost purring. If this was personal attention, she could take as much of it as he was willing to give.

He poured more shower gel over her breasts, teasing her nipples into tight points, then stroked lather over her ribcage, her belly. Lily quivered as he dropped to his knees in front of her. With his hair plastered back like that, he looked like a model for an expensive fragrance. Incredibly sexy. A gorgeous man with dark hair and a sensual mouth and olive skin and a regal air about him. The kind of man any woman would want to find in her shower.

He paid attention to her legs, next. Starting with the hollows of her ankles, he worked his way up her calves to the backs of her knees, then flattened his palms against her inner thighs, gently parting them. He looked up and gave her a look of pure desire, and her knees went weak; she had to hold onto his shoulders for balance. Karim lathered his hands again, then stroked between her legs, teasing her as he washed her. Every time his thumb brushed her clitoris, she quivered in anticipation. She knew he was doing it deliberately, increasing the pressure very slightly with each stroke; she tried to hold out, tried to be strong and not give in to the heavy, thudding pulse of desire.

But then Karim replaced his hand with his mouth, and Lily lost it completely, tipping her head back and climaxing hard as the water poured down on her. He held her close as her body tightened and relaxed, over and over again. And then, when the aftershocks had died away, he stood up again and stroked her hair back from her face.

'Sorry about that,' he said, looking not in the slightest bit repentant. 'I couldn't resist.'

'I…Karim.' She swallowed hard. 'That was amazing.'

'Good.'

She took a deep breath. 'My turn.'

'That's not the way it works. You don't have to return the favour. Not right now.' His eyes glittered. 'Though I think you've just put a picture in my head that's going to stop me sleeping tonight.'

Sleep. Right now she felt boneless. She wanted to curl up next to him in that huge bed, under the white sheets, and go to sleep.

'So you like my shower?' he asked.

'It's amazing.' Just as he was.

He flicked a switch to turn it to waterfall mode. 'It's half the reason I bought this place. Maybe it's coming from a desert land…but I just love water.'

'I never knew bathrooms could be sexy.'

'It's a shower room. A wet room,' he corrected. 'My bathroom's different.' He gave her a slow, sexy smile, full of promise. 'And I'll introduce you to that another time.'

Another time.

Lily wasn't sure if it thrilled her or scared her more. Because now she'd shared the ultimate intimacy with him, she was very afraid that she was starting to fall for him. Harder and faster than she'd ever thought possible.

Karim switched off the water, then stepped out from the screens and pulled a towel from the railing, tucking it round his waist. Then he took another towel and wrapped her in it—the biggest, softest, thickest towel she'd ever touched. It felt like being wrapped in a cloud, she thought idly, tucking a corner of the towel under the top edge to keep it in place.

He groaned. 'Not good. You look way too sexy like that. Like Cleopatra wrapped in a carpet.' His amber eyes glittered. 'It makes me want to unwrap you and carry you back to my bed.'

Sexy? When she'd just stepped out of the shower? She looked at him in surprise. 'My hair's in rats' tails and I've probably got panda eyes.'

'Your hair's fine and you're not wearing any make up.'

Probably his shower had got rid of it all, she thought. She squeezed water out of her hair. 'Do you have another towel, please?'

'Sure.' He passed her a hand towel; she wrapped her hair in it, turban-style.

'Lily.' He smiled. 'It's the wrong name for you—you're not a snooty hothouse flower. You're more like an English wild flower.'

'What, like a bluebell? Hmm. Bluebell Finch.' She laughed. 'Now there's a name. It sounds more like the sort of thing a farmer would call his favourite cow.' She grinned. 'Moo.'

He laughed back. 'You crazy woman. That's not what I meant at all.' He pulled her into his arms and spun her round so they were both facing the mirror; then he wrapped his arms round her waist and bent slightly so he could press his cheek to hers. 'What I meant is that you're natural and warm. There's no artifice with you. You look as good without make up as you do wearing it.'

'I'll have you know, I spent *ages* doing my make up this morning. Trying to make myself look professional.'

'You looked professional, all right. But I still wanted to take all your clothes off, the second I saw you.' He untucked the corner of her towel. 'Just as I do now.' He held her gaze in the mirror; the heat in his eyes made her knees feel weak.

'Do you really have nothing to do, this afternoon?'

'Are you telling me that you do?'

'It's rude to answer a question with a question.'

He laughed. 'Right now, I can't think of anything more important than taking you back to bed.'

She leaned back against him and placed her hand over his, stilling it. 'These business meetings of yours—how soon are they?'

'They start at the end of the month.'

'Which gives us two weeks,' she said thoughtfully. 'Then if you want me to cater for you, O esteemed client, we have work to do. Starting now.'

He blinked. 'What sort of work?'

'Planning.' Her fingers burrowed underneath his, retrieved the corner of the towel and tucked it back into place. 'So I suggest we get dressed.'

His lips quirked. 'You're bossing me about?'

'As you told me earlier, we're in my country, not yours. So I don't have to obey your royal orders.'

'What happened to the customer always being right?'

'The customer,' Lily retorted, 'often needs a bit of guidance to get what they really want instead of what they *think* they want.'

'That's profound.'

'Actually, it's true,' she said. 'Oh, and I'll need to borrow some paper and a pen.'

He blinked. 'You plan the old-fashioned way?'

'No, but I don't have my laptop with me. Unless,' she said thoughtfully, 'maybe you have one I can borrow, so I can work on it and email my notes to myself? That would save us both a bit of time.'

'No problem. I'll set it up for you.'

'Thank you.' She paused. 'Karim, I'm not going to be able to work if you're walking about half naked.'

'Are you saying I'll distract you?' he teased.

'You know perfectly well you will.' She eyed the reflection of the shower. 'And I'm going to need some coffee if I'm to have a hope in hell of concentrating, after what you did to me in there.'

A corner of his mouth quirked. 'You approve of my shower, then?'

'If we don't get out of this room right now,' she said, 'I could be very tempted to drag you back under there. And put it in waterfall mode. And I'd have you with your back flat against those tiles, seeing stars instead of water.'

'I do hope that's a promise.'

Desire coiled in her belly. 'It is.'

'May I point out that you're the one who tucked that towel back round you and said we had to work?' he said mildly.

'It's a woman's privilege to change her mind.' She closed her eyes. 'Uh. Take your hands off me, and go and get dressed, before you derail my mind completely.'

He laughed, releasing her. 'All right, *habibti*. I'll put some clothes on, and then I'll go and make us some coffee while you're dressing.'

'*English* coffee?' she asked hopefully.

'Yes, English coffee.'

Lord, he was gorgeous when he smiled like that. He had

dimples. Cute, cute dimples. And it took all her will power to stop herself ripping off her towel and grabbing him.

'May I borrow a comb, please?'

'Sure.' He fished a comb out of a narrow drawer within the granite slab, and gestured to the built-in shelving at the side of the mirror above the basin. 'Help yourself to anything else you need.' He dipped his head and kissed the curve between her neck and her shoulder, his mouth warm and soft against her skin. 'And I'm going now, before I start letting you change my mind. Because once isn't enough, Lily. Not nearly enough.'

When Lily had finished dressing and came down to the kitchen, her hair damp but presentable, Karim was already there, having cleared up and made coffee. His clothes were crumpled; although he should've looked scruffy, he looked incredibly sexy.

'I'm probably going to regret asking this,' he said, 'but what are you thinking?'

'You. Rumpled,' she said economically.

He laughed. 'If you have a problem with that, I'll change.'

'Not a problem exactly.' She cleared her throat. 'You look as if you've just got out of bed.' And she wanted to take him back there again.

'Strictly speaking,' he said, 'it was the shower. I was too—um—distracted to tell you earlier, but the third door along the corridor is the guest suite. There are toiletries there, should you need them. Body lotion and what have you.'

She could imagine him smoothing body lotion into her skin, the way he'd lathered her in the shower. And he must have noticed her mouth parting, because colour slashed across his cheekbones. '*Habibti*, don't. You'll wreck my good intentions.'

'Coffee,' she said. 'We need coffee.' She dared not suggest a cold shower. Not after what he'd done to her under the spray.

'I'd rather take all your clothes off again.' He looked at the granite-topped table and then straight at her. 'I have a pomegranate in the fridge.'

Her train of thought followed his, and she could imagine herself spread naked on the table, pomegranate seeds trailed down her body—and he'd eat them one by one, slowly, until she was so hot and wet for him that...

'Coffee.' His voice had dropped an octave. 'And I think you'd better take your cup off the worktop yourself. Because if I touch you—even if it's just your fingers brushing against mine as you take the cup from me—I don't think I can be held responsible for my actions.'

Lily dragged in a breath, fighting to get herself under control. 'I don't do this sort of thing, Karim. I never behave like this. It isn't *me*.'

'I know. Hayley said you're married to your kitchen. You're focused on your career.' He took a swig of coffee, then swore softly in Arabic. 'This isn't helping. At all. For five years now I've played hard—but I've worked harder, and I've always managed to keep work and my social life entirely separate. Right now I couldn't give a damn about business. I want to take you back to my bed.'

'You're the one who mentioned the pomegranate.'

'Go in the living room. Now. And don't sit anywhere near me,' he warned, 'because I seem to have mislaid my self-control temporarily.'

By the time they sat down in his living room—he'd moved a low table and set up his laptop on it for her—they were both back in control. Almost.

'So, these meetings—bearing in mind you're talking to me under client confidentiality now, can you give me any idea what you're doing? Simply because I want to make the food work for you,' Lily said, 'and I'll have a better idea if I know where it fits in.'

He leaned back against the sofa opposite her. 'Client confidentiality?'

'I can sign an agreement, if you'd rather. But I hope over

the last few days you've got to know me well enough to believe that whatever you tell me stays with me. I need background information to help me plan the right sort of menu. I wouldn't serve the same kind of thing at a buffet for, say, financiers as I would for people who worked in the arts.'

'Why not?'

'Because financiers don't look at what they're eating, and people in the arts do—they notice colour and styling, so it has to be a bit more intricate to look at,' she explained.

'I see.'

'And I'm assuming that you want something special rather than the kind of sandwiches you could just ask the local deli to deliver.'

He was silent for so long that she was beginning to wonder if he'd changed his mind. And then he seemed to come to a decision. 'All right. My father's put me in charge of developing tourism and investment in Harrat Salma.'

'And that's why these people are coming? Because they'll invest or build hotels or what have you?'

'Yes. I've hand-picked them over the last few months—people whose work I like and whose beliefs fit with mine. People who believe in more than just a profit; people who'll put something back as well as taking it. I want them to use local people, local expertise—engineers and builders and the like—in the designs, and I want local people running the hotels, too.'

'So tell me about Harrat Salma,' she said. 'Work on the basis that I know absolutely nothing—apart from the fact it has deserts and volcanoes.'

He smiled. 'There's a lot more to my country than that. We're not one of the oil-rich states, but we do have a large mining industry—zinc, copper and gemstones. My people have a very long tradition of craftsmanship.'

She gestured to the wall hangings. 'Such as these?'

'And carpets, of course.' He raised an eyebrow. 'Not flying ones—sadly, they're a myth—but beautiful hand-woven silk ones.' He indicated the one in the centre of the room. 'Plus met-alwork, jewellery, sculpture. We have ancient sites, we have museums, we have marine heritage. We have the souks—the spice market, the silk market, the fruit and vegetable market where you haggle with the traders over mint tea; and we even have ultra-modern malls for Western visitors who can't live without their global stores. But I want our tourism to be as carbon-neutral as possible.'

'So you're going for the Green bandwagon.'

'It's nothing to do with bandwagons.' His eyes narrowed slightly. 'I want to look at harnessing geothermal energy. It's not a bandwagon, Lily—it's just common sense and using our gifts wisely. We have a very special landscape, and it deserves conserving. And I will not permit dune-bashing. It's popular in some of our neighbouring countries, but in Harrat Salma it's absolutely out,' he asserted between clenched teeth.

She'd never heard him sound so haughty or so regal. For a brief moment, anger blazed in his eyes, and then it was damped down and he was back under control.

Part of her knew it was a dangerous question, given his reaction. But she asked it anyway. 'What's dune-bashing?'

'Taking a four-wheel drive up to the top of a dune and going straight down again—it's like white-water rafting on sand.'

The way he described it sounded as if it was something he'd once done—and maybe enjoyed. 'Sounds like a white knuckle ride in a natural theme park, to me. The kind of people who can afford to do that would definitely bring money into the country.'

'Along with no respect whatsoever—for the land or for my people. Not to mention the damage it can do.'

That sounded like the voice of bitter experience. Or someone so passionately committed to his country that he wanted to wrap it in cotton wool, at the same time as knowing that he needed to open it up to the world in order for his country to move forward.

'We don't need that kind of tourist.'

'So what kind of tourists do you want?'

'People who'll appreciate the traditional craftsmanship of our boats instead of demanding outboard motors. People who'll be content to dive and see the fish in their natural habitat rather than catch them for sport and throw them away. People who'll take the slow route to enjoy the landscape, on camels and on foot— a kind of desert safari—and listen to the stories of the guides.'

'People who'd want to spend a night sleeping outside in a volcano?' she asked with a smile.

He smiled wryly. 'Climbers and geologists, yes. I had thought to I—' He stopped abruptly.

'You'd thought to what?' she asked.

'Never mind. It's not important.'

His face had gone shuttered again, she noticed, so he wasn't being quite honest with her. It was important, all right: he just didn't want to talk about it. Like the dune-bashing thing; she was pretty sure there was more to it than simply conservation issues.

Though pushing him to talk about it when he was clearly unwilling really wasn't going to help her plan the menus. The best way she could help him, right now, was to do her job. And maybe he'd open up to her more when he'd relaxed again. 'So the people at your meetings are what, owners of tourist companies?'

'Specialist tourist companies,' he explained. 'I'm looking to do exclusive deals for the different areas—one for the diving and marine-based holidays, one for the desert safari trips, one for historical and educational tours, one for climbers. And another for those who'll invest in hotels.'

'Right.' She typed in some notes. 'Did you have anything in mind, food-wise? A sit down meal, a finger buffet, a fork buffet? And I assume you're looking to use traditional cuisine from your country rather than English food?'

'You're the expert, there,' he said, surprising her. 'What would you recommend?'

'I'd say do a fork buffet—and fusion food. Similar to the kind of food you cooked me, served a little warmer, and maybe with some slightly more English accompaniments. To give them a taste of the traditional, and yet at the same time show them your country has a modern outlook and welcomes those from other cultures,' she said.

'I like your take on that. Sounds good.'

'I'll also need to know if any of your guests have food allergies, and if any are vegetarian or vegan. Oh—and you'd better serve English coffee, not Arabic.'

He smiled wryly. 'I thought you might say that.'

'But you can offer a choice of your traditional mint tea as well as English tea. And the orange-and-mint concoction you made me—that'd go down really well.' She thought rapidly. 'At coffee break in the morning, I'll do you pastries to go with the coffee. Little ones that you can eat in one bite, including traditional pastries from Harrat Salma. Are Arabic pastries as sweet as Greek and Egyptian ones?'

'One of the most famous is *baklawa*,' he said. 'You may be more familiar with the Greek version of the pastry; in my country we add orange blossom water or rose water to the syrup.'

'But it'd still be very sweet,' she said thoughtfully. 'So I need to balance that with some not-so-sweet mouthfuls. OK. Give me a rundown of the kind of food people eat in your country.'

As he spoke she typed rapidly, occasionally stopping him to check spelling or ingredients. And finally she saved the file. 'Right. This will be a good basis for my research. I'll sort out some menus to run by you tomorrow, and I need to do a test run on the actual cuisine—not because I don't think I can do it, but because some of these dishes are new to me and I want to get the balance right before your meetings. Are you busy on Wednesday night?'

'Nothing I can't move.'

'Good. You're having a dinner party.'

'A dinner party?' he queried.

'Not the sort where you pay back social invitations, sit down and chat. I want you to invite your closest friends. People you trust. People who'll be willing to try a lot of different dishes, and give you an honest opinion on it.'

'Rafiq,' he suggested.

'Fine, but he's from your country. Can you invite someone English as well, so I can have a view from someone who doesn't know your culinary traditions?'

'How many are you looking for?'

'You, Rafiq and two more.'

'Luke. My best friend. *If* I can drag him away from work.' He paused. 'Did you want me to invite anyone female?'

'Women do own and run hotels and tourism companies,' she pointed out. 'Or aren't they allowed to do that in Harrat Salma?'

He smiled. 'Of course they are. It's not a backward country.'

'Sorry, I didn't mean to imply it was.' She gave him a rueful smile. 'But our cultures are different.'

'Yes. And I suppose you do have a point. Women are educated in my country and they can work if they choose to do so.' He paused. 'Except for the women in my family, of course.'

'Why "of course"?'

He frowned. 'Because it isn't appropriate for royal women to work for someone else.'

'I can see that, but couldn't they run their own business?'

'No.'

'Why not?'

'Because they have diplomatic duties. It's exactly the same for the men.' He shrugged. 'Maybe we can invite Cathy, then.'

'Cathy?'

'She's the head of the café in Luke's new health club. And he offered to lend me her services.'

'Did he, now,' she said dryly.

He raised an eyebrow. 'He knew I was in a jam—and you'd turned me down, at that point.'

'A jam?'

'Did you really think I'm that disorganised, *habibti*, that I'd set up meetings and not have all the details covered well beforehand? I had a caterer. But family circumstances meant that she had to let me down. Which is why it's all a last-minute rush now.'

'Didn't she organise a replacement before she left?'

Karim spread her hands. '*Habibti*, if your sister needed you badly, wouldn't you drop everything to help her?'

'I'm an only child.'

He inclined his head. 'Your mother, then.'

'Yes, of course I would. But I also wouldn't leave my clients in a mess.'

'What if it was an emergency, and you didn't have time to sort things out?'

'I'd *make* time.'

He gave her a sidelong look. 'You're hard on people.'

'I'm not. But I give my best. I expect others to do the same for me.'

'Noted,' he said dryly.

But it was still bugging her. 'So your friend Luke sorted out your problem for you—but you've decided to drop this Cathy for me?'

'Nothing of the kind,' he said, lifting his chin. 'I haven't spoken to Cathy yet. I was planning to give you until Wednesday—and only if I hadn't persuaded you to cook for me by then did I intend to take up Luke's offer.'

'Well, I've agreed to cook for you now.' She moistened her lower lip. 'Though I don't mix business and pleasure.'

'Neither do I,' Karim said. 'But I'm breaking the rules as of now.' He moved to sit beside her, took her hand and kissed the pulse beating madly in her wrist. 'And so are you.'

'Temporarily. I'm your temporary cook, and your temporary…'

'Lover,' he said, and traced a path of kisses up her forearm.

He'd reduced her to a quivering pile of mush—almost. But there was one thing she needed to be sure about. 'Ground rules,' she said.

He nibbled the sensitive spot in her inner elbow. 'Rules?'

'Just one.' One that was really important to her. Even though she wasn't going to get involved with him. 'And it's a deal-breaker.'

That got his attention. He released her arm and looked straight at her. 'What's that?'

'While you're with me, no harem.'

He frowned. 'I've dated a lot, though it's always been one woman at a time. I'd never dishonour my girlfriends by doing otherwise.'

Now she'd offended him. Maybe she should explain…but she couldn't bring herself to tell him about Jeff. To let him know what a fool she'd been. 'Just checking,' she said. She took a deep breath. 'And I think you'd better go and sit back over there. Before you make me delete this lot accidentally. Like I did with my article, the other day.'

'I distract you?' he teased, but to her relief he did as she asked.

'You know damn well you do.'

'If it makes you feel any better,' he said, 'it's mutual. So. Ground rules. Number one, this is temporary. Number two, while we're seeing each other, neither of us will see anyone else. And number three, we keep our work together entirely separate from our private life.'

'Agreed,' she said, adding a private rule just for herself. Number four, no getting involved. This was going to be just for fun. Sex. Spectacular sex.

She flicked into his email program and emailed herself the notes she'd just made. 'Well, now it's time to work. I have research to do and menus to plan, and you have people to invite to dinner. Seven o'clock sharp on Wednesday.'

'Fine.'

'And I—' she glanced at the clock on the computer '—need to be gone.'

'I'll drive you back,' he said.

She shook her head. 'No need. I'll take the Tube. And don't argue, Karim. I'm perfectly capable of seeing myself home. I'm twenty-eight, not sixteen.'

'The offer's there if you change your mind.'

'I think,' she said softly, 'if you saw me home, I'd feel obliged to invite you in for coffee. And there's the small matter of you and me and, um, granite.'

His gaze went hot. 'Are there any pomegranates in your fridge?'

'No.' She sucked in a breath. 'Though there might be, tomorrow.'

'Then I'll see you tomorrow, *habibti*.' He dipped his head and kissed her lightly. 'Mid afternoon.'

'Business,' she reminded him.

He took her hand and rubbed the pad of his thumb over her palm. 'Business *first*,' he said softly. 'And then…pomegranates.'

CHAPTER NINE

'THAT'S two Mondays on the trot I've beaten you at squash now,' Luke said, 'and I've barely even broken a sweat tonight. This isn't good. It isn't good at all.' He spread his hands. 'But at least this week you're looking a bit happier. So are you going to fill me in on what's happened?'

'Lily agreed to cook for me,' Karim said.

Luke groaned. 'Please tell me you're not letting your libido rule your brain.'

'I'm not.' Much. 'Anyway. I need you on Wednesday night.'

'Need me for what?'

'Dinner. My place. And is there any chance you can bring Cathy?'

Luke frowned. 'I thought you just said Lily agreed to cook for you?'

'She has. But she wants to do a trial run of the food—and she wants some guinea pigs who'll give her an honest opinion. Which means you...and a professional one from Cathy would be good.'

'I'll see if Cathy's free, but I can't guarantee it,' Luke said. 'For all I know, she might have a jealous other half.'

'Then get her to bring him—or her—as well.' Karim paused. 'How come you don't know much about Cathy, if she's in charge of the club's kitchen?'

'It's not on her CV, and it's against the law to ask,' Luke said economically. 'Anyway, it doesn't matter whether she's single or attached. She's good at her job. That's all I need to know.'

'Aren't you supposed to show an interest in your staff?' Karim asked mildly.

'No. And, unlike some people around here, I'm not stupid enough to think about getting involved with someone I work with.'

'I'm not thinking about getting involved with Lily.' Strictly speaking, that was true. He wasn't thinking about it—he already *was* involved with her. On a temporary basis. With mutually agreed ground rules.

Luke gave him a sceptical look. 'OK. I'll sort Wednesday.'

'It's not interfering with work?'

'Not really.' Luke shrugged. 'I'd been invited to a party. But I'm getting bored with parties. Being a guinea pig sounds a lot more fun.' He raised an eyebrow. 'And it has the added bonus of me getting to meet this woman who's turned you into a gibbering idiot.'

'That's an exaggeration. I'm not a gibbering idiot.'

'Hmm. I reserve the right to comment until after I've met her.'

Karim laughed. 'I wouldn't expect anything less from a man who calls a spade a "bloody shovel". Come on. As I lost, I'll get the drinks. And you can tell me all about this new scheme of yours.'

The following afternoon, Lily opened the door to Karim, who had a veritable armful of deep blue irises and pink and white tulips.

'What's this, an entire florist's?' she asked.

'Hello to you, too.' He leaned forward and kissed her lightly on the lips.

'Karim! This is meant to be business.'

'Not until three o'clock.' He glanced at his watch. 'And right now it's ten minutes to. Which means,' he said, putting the flowers in her arms and closing the door behind them, 'I have ten minutes to kiss you stupid.'

He was gratified to see how swiftly she blushed. Her eyes looked huge and her mouth had parted, already inviting the said kisses. Then she shook herself. 'I…Karim, thank you for the flowers. They're lovely. But this isn't going to work.'

'Yes, it is.' He marched her into the kitchen, took the flowers from her, put them on the draining board, and fiddled with her oven.

'What are you doing?'

'Setting the timer. We have nine minutes before our business meeting.' He blew her a kiss, and placed a brown paper bag on the worktop.

'I'm going to regret asking, but what's that?' she asked.

'Pomegranate. In case you were out of stock. Stop talking, Lily, you're wasting time. Eight and a half minutes.' He pulled her into his arms and kissed her. Thoroughly. Until she was kissing him back and made no protest whatsoever when his hands burrowed under the hem of her camisole top to stroke her midriff and then unclip her bra.

He loved touching Lily. Kissing her. Loved the warmth of her response and the fact that she didn't hold back—she'd untucked his shirt and was teasing his skin with her fingertips, the same way he was teasing her, drawing lazy circles on the soft undercurves of her breasts.

Karim was just unzipping her jeans, ready to ease them down over her hips, when the oven timer pinged. For a moment, he considered ignoring it—but the sound was loud enough to break his concentration. Enough to remind him that he needed to prove to Lily that they could manage the fine line between business and pleasure.

He switched off the timer, then restored order to Lily's delightfully déshabillé clothes and tucked his own shirt back in place. 'Right. Menus.'

'Karim, I—' She sounded dazed.

He laughed. 'Your body's definitely out to lunch, *habibti*. And I think your mind might be, too. Where did my clever, competent cook go?'

'Let's just say you achieved your objective,' she said wryly.

'What?'

'You just kissed me stupid.' She laughed. 'Or maybe I should say, you just kissed me, stupid.'

'Playing punctuation games with me, are you, Miss Finch?' And he loved her fencing with him like this. 'I'm going to kiss you a lot more, later,' he promised. 'After our meeting. So where are we sitting?'

'You,' she said, 'are not sitting anywhere near me. I need a cold shower.'

'Mmm. *Shower*.' He looked speculatively at her. 'How would you rate your shower in comparison to mine?'

'One out of ten. Don't even think about it.' She tidied her hair, then went over to the kitchen sink and splashed her face with cold water before drying it on a towel. 'And don't do that again.'

'Do what?'

'Distract me when we're talking business.'

'We weren't talking business,' he reminded her. 'Our appointment was mid-afternoon—and I was early.'

'You're splitting hairs. So have you sorted out your guests for Wednesday?'

'Rafiq, Luke, probably Cathy, maybe Cathy's jealous boyfriend.'

'There's a jealous boyfriend involved?'

He shrugged. 'Luke has no idea. Could be a husband. Could be nobody.'

She groaned. 'This friend of yours sounds very like you. Focused on work and nothing else penetrates your consciousness.'

Karim laughed. 'He's not a sheikh. He's a barrow boy.'

'I thought you said he owned a gym?'

'Several, actually. Oh, wait. I think he might have sold most of them. The new one's just because he was bored waiting for another project to get going.'

'He bought a gym because he was *bored*?' Lily blinked, as if unable to take it in. 'Why?'

'Because it was on its last legs, and he saw it as a challenge—to see how quickly he could turn it around.'

'You mean, he's an asset stripper? Buys things and sells them again almost immediately?'

'He buys failing businesses and turns them around and sells them as going concerns,' Karim corrected. 'And he's very, very good at what he does. He's loaded, although he started out with a single market stall. He also had the best brain on my MBA course.' He raised an eyebrow. 'Luke managed to talk his way onto the course with no qualifications whatsoever.'

She gave him a level stare. 'If you're talking about degrees, I didn't go to university, either. There's nothing wrong with that.'

'I didn't say there was—and, frankly, in your line of business, it's experience and flair that counts, not paper qualifications.'

She coughed. 'I didn't say I had no paper qualifications. Of course I do. I studied while I got practical work experience.'

'So when did you decide to go it alone?' he asked curiously.

Now there was a question and a half. 'I set up Amazing Tastes four years ago,' she answered carefully. Karim didn't need to know about before.

'Brave move.'

'I enjoy a challenge.'

He gestured towards the brown paper bag. 'There's your challenge for today.'

'No,' she said firmly. 'Do you want a coffee while we're discussing menus?'

'Yes, please.'

'Then go and sit down.' She shooed him over to her conservatory, and put the flowers in water while she waited for the kettle to boil. She had just enough vases to contain them all, but it was a close-run thing. A completely over-the-top gesture, and one she should've disapproved of—but she loved the fact that he'd bought her so many beautiful spring flowers. Especially the irises, because he'd clearly remembered how much she loved blue flowers.

She took two mugs of coffee over to the conservatory and set them on the table, and made sure she sat opposite him—far enough away so they couldn't actually touch—before talking him through the menus she'd devised.

'Sounds good to me,' he said when she'd finished. 'So how does the catering work? Do you cook it here and bring it over, or do you have the ingredients delivered to my place and cook there?'

'I bring the ingredients to your place,' she said. 'Unless it's something that needs to be prepared well in advance, I prefer to cook everything fresh at my client's. And your kitchen's as good as mine.' She grinned. 'I'll bring my own knives and pans, though.'

'How do you know mine aren't good enough?'

'Apart from the fact I'm used to working with mine, they're the tools of my trade…and I'm fussy.'

'I'll remember that.' He paused. 'Actually, some of those dishes do need to be prepared well in advance. Preferably the day before, so they have time to marinade and let the flavours develop.'

She coughed. 'You once told me you believed in letting your staff get on with their job without interference.'

'I do. But you're not my staff.'

'You're paying me to do a job, which amounts to the same thing.'

'Not for tax purposes, it doesn't. You're not my employee.'

'Don't split hairs. You know what I mean. And you're interfering.'

'And whose country's cuisine are we talking about?' he fenced.

'Not yours *or* mine,' she said tartly. 'This is fusion food. It's designed to give people a taste of your country while also making them feel at home here.'

'Fine. What time do you need access to the kitchen?'

She looked at him. 'Oh. I assumed that you worked from your flat. Your dining room's a lot like a boardroom.'

'I do, and it is,' he said. 'Don't worry, I won't be under your feet while you're working.'

'Your kitchen will be completely out of bounds,' she warned. 'It'll be my work area. And I don't like being interrupted when I'm working.'

He grinned. 'So you're one of these temperamental chefs who swears a lot and hits people with a frying pan, are you?'

She laughed back. 'Hardly. But I'm serious, Karim. If you want me to do a good job, you need to give me the space to do it.'

'I'll be completely professional,' he said. 'So what's the plan for tomorrow?'

'I'll arrive at ten. I'll be bringing my van.'

'Fine. Park outside and call me—Rafiq will take your equipment up to the flat and park your van in the secure parking underneath the complex.' He smiled. 'Now that's all sorted…come and sit with me.'

'This is business.'

'We've finished business. This is you and me,' he corrected. 'So either you come here and sit on my lap…or I'll come over to you.'

'What, you're going to sit on *my* lap?' she teased.

'Now you're stretching my patience, woman. Enough.' He stood up, walked over to her, scooped her off the chair and sat down in her place, settling her on his lap.

'You're just a caveman at heart,' she accused.

'And your point is?'

Before she had the chance to answer, he kissed her. Thoroughly.

'So. Now we've agreed that,' he said, 'what are you doing for the rest of the day?'

'Writing my shopping list for tomorrow morning. I'm using as much organic stuff as possible, by the way,' she said.

'Fine.' He nibbled his way along her jawline. 'I'd love to take you out to dinner tonight.'

She could hear the 'but', and said it for him.

He sighed. 'I have a tedious meeting to attend.'

'You mean, you're going to a party,' she said dryly.

He nodded. 'Though I'll be leaving early.' He paused. 'Maybe I could come and see you on the way home.'

'That depends on your definition of early.'

'You're planning an early night?' He smiled. 'Good. I like the sound of that.'

Did he mean he was thinking of joining her? Was he inviting himself to stay overnight? This was moving way too fast for her. 'Karim, we can't do this.'

'Yes, we can. And don't argue. We both know all I have to do is kiss you.'

She scowled. 'That's arrogant.'

'Maybe, but it's also true.'

It was, and that made things worse.

'If it makes you feel any better,' he said softly, 'you put my head in a spin as well.'

Maybe, she thought, but not enough of a spin to ask me to go to the party with you. And even though she knew he looked on it as a business networking opportunity—which meant he'd be busy and she couldn't be there to distract him—it still rankled. So she ignored his comment. 'You'll need to prepare for your "tedious" party. And I need to prepare things for tomorrow.'

'You have a point. And I'm not going to encroach on your professional time. Though I reserve the right to encroach on your other time.' He kissed her lightly. 'Thank you, *habibti*.'

'What for?'

'Understanding that my job isn't just nine to five.'

She felt the colour rush into her face. She hadn't exactly been understanding. She'd been sulking and thinking like a jealous girlfriend—which she had no right to do, because she wasn't officially his girlfriend and they'd agreed that their relationship was temporary. Even crosser with herself, she slid off his lap. 'I'll see you tomorrow.'

He smiled. 'Bring the pomegranate with you.' He stood up, and she saw him out; though she found, once her shopping list was done, she couldn't really settle to anything.

This wasn't good. Wasn't good at all. She'd promised herself, after Jeff, that she'd never let anyone distract her from her business again. And what was she doing? Mooning around after a playboy who'd already made it clear to her that they had no future. So much for thinking that she could handle this.

Later that evening, her mobile phone beeped. She flicked into the text screen and realised the message was from Karim.

*Party **extremely** tedious, food nowhere near as good as yours.*

Good, she texted back.

Tomorrow's too far away. Can I call in on my way home?

Too, too tempting. *No. Am going to sleep now.*

Two seconds later, the phone rang. 'You're in bed?' Karim asked. 'What are you wearing?'

She sucked in a breath. 'Karim, you're in a public place! You can't have this kind of conversation with me.'

'Yes, I can—I'm in the foyer outside and nobody can hear me. I excused myself to make a business call.'

'Even so—Karim, we're not having this conversation.'

He laughed softly. 'Chicken. Don't you want to have phone sex with me?'

Oh-h-h. Even the suggestion made her wet. 'I'm not a chicken,' she said primly. 'I'm being sensible.'

'How about I tell you what I'm wearing?' he suggested.

'No.'

'I could always tell you about my bath…' His voice was full of amusement, and she could imagine that sexy mouth smiling. That sexy mouth working against her skin, teasing her into arousal…

'*No,*' she said firmly. 'I'll see you tomorrow at ten.'

'Then goodnight, *habibti*. Pleasant dreams.'

'Goodnight,' she said, but she was smiling when she put the phone down again.

CHAPTER TEN

FIRST thing the next morning, Lily did the shopping, so her ingredients were the freshest they could possibly be. Then she drove over to Karim's flat, called him as arranged, and allowed Rafiq to carry her bags up to the flat and park her van in the car park beneath the complex.

'Good morning, *habibti*.' Karim opened the door. 'Now, are you Miss Finch or Lily today?'

She rolled her eyes. 'Lily, of course—but I'm here on business.'

He glanced at his watch. 'Actually, you're two minutes early. Which means you can kiss me hello.'

She'd barely uttered the first syllable of his name in protest before he kissed her. A warm, sweet and promising kiss that made her knees weak. And then he closed the door behind her. 'Right. Do you have everything you need?'

'I'm pretty sure I do.'

'Good. Rafiq is at your disposal, should you need anything. His number is on speed dial on the kitchen phone—dial hash then three.' He ushered her through to the kitchen. 'And I'll be next door, if you need any input from me.'

'Sure. Want me to bring you a coffee when I make myself one?'

He smiled at her. 'You are indeed a woman whose price is above rubies. Thanks. I'd appreciate that.'

She changed into her chef's whites and settled into the

kitchen, spreading out her equipment and working through the first part of her list. When she'd sorted out everything that needed marinating and the first batch of bite-size Arabic short-bread was out of the oven, she made coffee and carried a mug and a plate through to Karim in the next room.

He was working on a spreadsheet on his laptop when she walked in. She'd never seen him at work before, and it was a revelation. He looked focused, brooding, intense—and sexy as hell. His face was all strong angles and planes, and with his hair raked back rather than flopping over his forehead he looked slightly forbidding rather than the teasing playboy she was used to.

He looked up and his eyes crinkled at the corners. 'Hello, *habibti*. How's it going?'

'Fine. You?'

'Fine.' His eyes widened as he spotted the shortbread. 'Is that for me?'

'It's still fairly warm and it's an early test. Client's privilege.' She smiled at him. 'I know I told you the kitchen was out of bounds, but with the rest of my clients I'm happy for them to come in and chat to me and taste things whenever they want.'

His eyes narrowed. 'So why can't I do the same?'

'Number one, you're busy. Number two, you'd distract me. So. The kitchen ban stays.'

He tried the shortbread and closed his eyes in seeming bliss for a moment. 'This is fabulous, Lily. If you ever decide you want to work in a warmer climate, you'd command premium prices as a pastry chef in my country.' He looked appreciatively at her. 'If the rest of the food's like this, you'll have done half my job for me.'

'It's really too early to say. Wait until you try the rest,' she said. 'But I'm glad you like it, so far.' On impulse, she leaned over and kissed the tip of his nose—and backed out of reach before he could react.

'You just broke the rules again, Miss Finch,' he said thoughtfully. 'Which means the kitchen is no longer out of bounds.'

'Oh, yes, it is.' She held both hands up in a 'stop' gesture. 'Stay!' she said, laughing, and fled back to the kitchen.

She was busy working on a rose-water cream filling, with everything else ticking over nicely, when Karim wandered into the kitchen. 'It's half past one. Do you want me to make you a sandwich or something?'

'It's sweet of you to offer, but no—and this room is supposed to be out of bounds,' she reminded him.

'*Habibti*, you've been on the go since you got here—surely you need to sit down and take a break?'

She shook her head. 'It's not like that in a kitchen. When I'm cooking, I work through.'

'Hmm. I don't want to be a slave driver.'

'You're not. I'm setting my own pace,' she reassured him. 'But if you're desperate to help, I'll let you set up the dining table later. I need all four of you on one side of that enormous table, and a big runner in the middle so I can set the dishes on it.'

'Of course. Do you mind if I make myself a sandwich?'

'I'll do it.'

He frowned. 'Lily, you're busy. I really don't expect you to wait on me as well as everything else.'

'It's fine. Don't fuss. Now, shoo,' she said with a smile. 'I'll bring you something through in a couple of minutes.'

She made Karim a sandwich and herself a mug of coffee, and carried on. The rest of the afternoon whizzed by; at five o'clock, she stopped for just long enough to take him a sample of the *baklawa* she'd made and a cup of very English tea.

'These are absolutely perfect,' he pronounced. He gave her a teasing sidelong glance. 'Dare I ask, given that the media has this thing about saving time at the moment…did you make the pastry yourself as well as the filling and the syrup?'

She gave him a speaking look. 'What do you think?'

'I think I've just insulted you. Of course you didn't cut corners. You're a consummate professional, Miss Finch.'

She inclined her head in acknowledgement. 'Thank you. I'm nearly there.'

'Let me know when you want me to set up the room. I take it you're joining us?'

'Not to eat, no. With the amount of stuff I've tasted,' she explained, 'I'm too stuffed to face a meal.'

'You're the boss, *habibti*.'

At five to seven, Karim's guests arrived. 'Lily, this is Luke and Cathy—Rafiq you already know.'

'Good to meet you,' Lily said. 'And thanks for being guinea pigs tonight.'

'Pleasure,' Luke said.

Cathy just stared, open-mouthed. 'You're Elizabeth Finch! I recognise you from your picture in *Modern Life* magazine.' She nudged her boss. 'Luke, why didn't you tell me *Elizabeth Finch* was cooking for us? Do you have any idea how much of a legend she is?'

'Karim told me Lily cooks for the rich and famous, not that she *is* famous. And as I don't exactly read the same kind of magazines you do…' Luke spread his hands. 'Sorry.'

'Enough of the celeb stuff. Call me Lily, and I'm just the cook,' Lily said. 'And you're all here to work.' She ushered them over to the dining table. 'I've put some sheets there for you all to fill in, but if you'd rather tell me than write it down, that's fine. I want an honest opinion. Don't hold back. So if you like it, I want to know what you like about it, and if you don't, that's also fine: I need to know what the problem is, whether it's the texture or it's too spicy or it's too bland. That'll help me do the final tweaks and get the right balance for the final recipe.' She smiled at them. 'You're getting a lot of different dishes, a lot of different tastes, so I'll bring you sorbet to cleanse your palate between dishes.'

To her relief, the savoury dishes went down well—her testers suggested a few adjustments, but in the main she'd kept on the fine line she'd intended to tread.

Then she brought in the pastries. 'OK. We have filo pastries filled with rose-water cream, some traditional date-and-nut pastries, *baklawa*—which is like the Greek pastry but flavoured with rose water—Arabic shortbread, and semolina cookies stuffed with date and walnuts,' she said.

'And the little muffins?' Luke asked.

She looked straight at Karim. 'White chocolate—and pomegranate.'

'You are *so* going to pay for that,' Karim mouthed at her.

She just laughed and made them try every single one, with a mouthful of sorbet in between each.

'I love these shortbread biscuits. Is that orange blossom water you added?' Cathy asked.

'And egg yolk,' Lily said.

'Can I beg the recipe, please? And for the pomegranate muffins? They'd go down really well with the breakfast crowd at the gym.'

'Sure.' Lily smiled at her. 'I was thinking about adding a little grated orange rind to the muffins. It's a fairly classic combination—and orange mixed with pomegranate juice, olive oil and a little ground coriander makes a fabulous salad dressing.' She caught Karim's eye, and gave him a wicked smile, guessing exactly what was going through his head. The words 'pomegranate' and 'dressing' had definitely sparked off an idea.

She finished the tasting session with mint tea.

'This and those little semolina and date cookies,' Rafiq said, 'are as good as my mother's.'

'Thank you.' She acknowledged the compliment with a dip of her head, and gathered up the tasting notes, placing them in a folder and then putting the folder in a briefcase. 'And thank you all for being honest. I'll take your comments into account when I tweak the recipes before Karim's meetings.'

'I can see why you held out for her to be your caterer,' Luke said quietly to Karim at the doorway as he and Cathy left. 'She's very good at her job—the food was fabulous. And she's incredibly focused. She even managed to concentrate on talking to us and finding out what we really thought, when every time she looked at you it was obvious that she just wanted to rip all your clothes off and melt into your arms.'

'You don't have to do the "bloody shovel" bit,' Karim said, feeling the colour flare in his face.

Luke simply grinned. 'I like the way there's no side to her, no airs and graces—what you see is exactly what you get.'

'But?' Karim could see the word written all over his friend's face.

'You're still an idiot. She's lovely, but it's going to end in tears,' Luke warned. 'Mixing business and pleasure is a seriously bad idea.'

'We both know the score,' Karim said. 'She doesn't have room in her life for a relationship. And she knows that I have to go back to Harrat Salma. We have ground rules. It's not a problem.'

'I thought you said you weren't thinking about getting involved with her?'

'Technically, I wasn't thinking about it.'

Luke picked up exactly what he meant. 'You'd already done it. *Idiot*.' He sighed. 'Just be careful. Because one or both of you is going to get hurt.'

'No, we're not. We know what we're doing. Eyes wide open,' Karim insisted. 'It's going to be fine.'

His best friend didn't look convinced, but didn't press the point.

Rafiq, having offered to help clear up and been turned

down by Lily, headed for his own quarters. Which left Karim alone with Lily.

He walked into the kitchen, where she was clearing up.

'You,' he said, 'did an amazing job.'

She shrugged. 'I try to live up to the name of my business.'

'You definitely did, tonight.' He took the pan from her hand.

'I need to finish clearing up, Karim.'

'No. *Enough*,' he said softly. 'You've been on your feet all day. I'll sort it out.'

'It's part of my job.'

'I don't care. *I'm* doing it. And remember that the client is always right,' he said. 'And I could pull rank and remind you that, actually, I own this kitchen.' Then, when her expression turned mutinous, he leaned forward to kiss the tip of her nose. 'Lily, you need a break. Even if you don't think you do. Come on.' He took her hand and drew her towards the stairs.

'Where are we…?' She stopped.

'You,' he said, 'are going to chill out a bit while I finish clearing up.' He led her up the stairs and stopped outside the door next to his room. 'I promised to introduce you to my bathroom. One second.' He flicked a couple of switches, then opened the door. 'Come with me.'

She stopped and just stared.

If anything, the room was even more gorgeous than his wet room. The tiles here were stone, textured and matte rather than smooth and glossy; a huge potted kentia palm stood in one corner. There was a freestanding bath finished in dark grey stone in the centre of the room, uplit with an aqua wash—and she could hear music playing softly. It wasn't something she knew, but it was incredibly moving.

'Like it?' he asked.

'Love it,' she breathed. 'What's the music?'

'Very English, actually,' he said with a smile. 'Something I heard performed when I was at Cambridge, and it blew me away. It's Vaughan Williams' "Fantasia on a Theme of Thomas Tallis". Perfect for chilling out. Though if you'd rather have something else, I can change it.'

'No. It's gorgeous.'

There were fluffy white bath sheets hanging on the towel rail, and the basin was a frosted glass bowl resting on a dark grey slab. Toiletries were lined up neatly on a glass shelf, and there was a mirror above the sink.

But she was drawn back to the bath. It was big enough for two people, with a shelf on one side; the kind of place where you could lie back in a pile of bubbles and read a magazine, with a cup of tea beside you, Lily thought.

Utter, utter bliss.

Without another word, Karim leaned over the bath, flicked a switch so the plug sank down flush with the base of the bath, and ran the water.

The water flowing into the white interior of the bath was the same shade of aqua as the recessed lights under the bath.

'That's stunning. How did you…?' She gestured to the water.

'It's a tap light.'

When she drew closer, she realised that there was a beam of aqua-coloured light running through the water; the actual water in the bath was clear.

'Boys and their toys,' she said, rolling her eyes.

He grinned. 'You have to admit, it's seriously cool.'

'It's seriously cool,' she said. She glanced up at the ceiling.

'What?' he asked.

'I wondered if you had one of those glass roofs that turn clear so you can see the sky.'

He wrinkled his nose. 'There's no point, in London. You won't see anything other than an orange glow and the odd aeroplane. A hot tub under the desert sky, on the other hand…now, there it would be worth having a clear glass roof.'

She could just imagine it. And she could also imagine Karim in the bath with her, his wet hair slicked back from his face and his body easing into hers.

For a moment, she went dizzy and had to hold onto the side of the bath.

'Lily? Are you all right?'

'Just a bit tired,' she said, not wanting to admit how much he affected her.

'Hmm.' He tipped something from a small bottle into the water, and rich, lush bubbles began to form.

'Vanilla,' she said, sniffing the air, 'and…?'

He slanted her a look. 'Pomegranate.'

Ah-h-h.

She'd been teasing him about pomegranates all evening.

'Hmm. That word's a very effective way to shut you up,' Karim said thoughtfully. 'Though not half as much fun as this.' He spun her round and lowered his mouth to hers, then nibbled her lower lip until she opened her mouth and let him kiss her properly.

She shivered when he broke the kiss. 'Karim…'

'Humour me,' he said softly. 'You're tired. I want to give you a few minutes to relax.' He removed the Buff from her hair and ran his fingers through the thick tresses for a moment, letting it fall to her shoulders. Then he undid the buttons on her chef's jacket, so very slowly.

'Mmm. I wondered what you were wearing under this,' he said in approval as he saw her lacy white bra.

Her trousers were next. And by the time he'd finished undressing her, the bath was ready. He turned off the taps, tested the temperature of the water, then took off his watch and placed it on the granite surround by the glass bowl of the sink.

'What are you…?' she began.

He rolled up his sleeves and gently lifted her into the bath. 'Just lie back and relax. I'll bring you a drink in a minute.' He forestalled her protest with a kiss. 'No arguments. Your client demands it.'

Lily, realising just how tired she was, gave in.

This was bliss.

A deep, hot bath with lots of bubbles and the most gorgeous music… She lay back and closed her eyes.

She had no idea how much time passed before Karim returned, carrying an opened bottle of champagne and a champagne flute. In the bottom of the glass there was what looked like a hibiscus flower. As he poured the champagne into the glass the flower opened.

'Now that's showing off,' she said. 'But very pretty.'

He placed the bottle on the side of the bath, on the shelf she'd imagined with a cup of tea, and handed the glass to her.

She refused to accept it. 'That's a really lovely thought, but I can't—I have to drive home.'

'Actually, you don't have to,' he said. There was a long, long pause. 'You could—if you wished—stay here tonight. With me.'

Her heart missed a beat. 'Karim.'

'I know.' He smiled wryly. 'I can't believe I asked you, either. I've never invited anyone to stay here overnight before.'

'I…' She swallowed hard. She wanted to say yes. She really, really wanted to say yes. A whole night in Karim's arms.

But a practical voice in her head wouldn't let her do it. 'I don't have clean underwear with me,' she said, suddenly embarrassed.

'I have a washer-dryer. If I put your clothes in now, they'll be ready to wear in the morning.'

She blinked. 'I thought you said you used a laundry service?'

'I do. But I still have a washing machine.'

'But you're a pr—'

He touched his forefinger to her lips to silence the word. 'Forget about the wretched title, Lily. If I had to sit around until someone would come to dress me, like some Regency duke waiting for his valet, I'd get nothing done. I believe in taking responsibility for myself.' He let his hand drop. 'Stay with me tonight, Lily.'

Against her better judgement, she nodded.

He smiled. 'Good. And you can't change your mind any more—in about three minutes' time, all your clothes will be in my washing machine. Wet. And you'll have to wait at least until they're dry.' He scooped up her discarded clothing and disappeared.

She lay back and sipped the champagne. The bubbles burst against her tongue—a heady feeling, but nowhere near as heady as the feeling she got whenever Karim looked at her.

When he returned, he said nothing, but his gaze was very, very hot. He stripped efficiently, then took the glass from her hand and commanded softly, 'Move up.'

She shifted along the bath while he placed the glass on the shelf next to the bottle; he stepped in behind her, then scooped her onto his lap so that she lay back against him.

'That's better,' he murmured, wrapping one arm round her ribcage and kissing the curve of her neck. 'Much better.'

With his other hand, he retrieved the glass and took a sip, before holding it to her lips so that her mouth touched the place his had just left.

'I'm impressed by the hibiscus,' she said when he replaced the glass, tipping her head back so she could look up at him. 'Though I wondered if you were going to add pomegranate seeds.'

'Believe me, *habibti*, I thought about it,' he said. 'I'll save that for another time.'

'This is incredibly decadent. This huge bath, all these bubbles, and champagne, too.'

'Life,' he said, 'is for enjoying. Because it's way, way too short.'

Something in his tone told her that this was something that

went deep. The key to Karim—who he really was, under the playboy mask. She took his free hand, brought it up to her lips and pressed a kiss into his palm, then curled her fingers over it.

'Careful, *habibti*,' he warned, his voice slightly cracked. 'I'm tempted to do something very, very rash.'

And, with his erection pressing against her, she could guess just what.

The really scary thing was that she could be very tempted, too.

He kissed the curve of her neck. 'I think we need to move out of here. While I'm still able to think straight.' He shifted her off his lap, climbed out of the bath and wrapped a towel around himself, then lifted her out and wrapped her in a towel before carrying her to his bed.

He flicked a switch, and uplighters set into the floor bathed the room in the softest of lights; then he closed the curtains, let his towel fall to the floor and walked slowly, slowly over to the bed. Lily's breath caught in her throat: Karim was gorgeous. All male. And she wanted him more than she'd ever wanted anyone in her life before.

'So, Lily. Just you and me,' he said huskily.

'Just you and me,' she agreed.

'And tonight you're going to sleep in my arms.'

How long had it last been since she'd spent the night in someone's arms? Years. She hadn't wanted to—not until now.

And she was absolutely sure she wasn't making the same mistake she'd made with Jeff. The situation was different. And Karim at least was a man of honour.

His lovemaking was tender and sweet and brought tears to her eyes. And as his body curled round hers, making her feel warm and safe, Lily drifted off to sleep, feeling more content and fulfilled than she had in a long, long time.

CHAPTER ELEVEN

THE next week and a half went by in a blur of cooking and planning and double-checking lists; Karim, too, was busy planning and fine-tuning his presentations.

And then Karim's intense schedule of business meetings began. Lily was at his flat early every morning to sort out the food and brief the waiting staff, then on her usual catering days she drove back via Hannah's in the afternoon, collecting the shopping ready for the evening's work.

By the end of the fortnight, she was ready to drop. But she still managed to celebrate with Karim on the Monday night, when he told her just how well everything had gone. 'And the food was a real talking point. It got them thinking about the tastes of my country, the new combined with the familiar,' he said. 'So, thanks to you, it's been a success.'

'It was just trappings,' Lily said. 'You're the one who came up with the statistics and the forecasts. You're the one who's worked out all the opportunities. And you're the one who sold those opportunities.'

'Teamwork,' Karim said. 'Credit where it's due.'

After that his schedule went crazy. The networking lunches and parties morphed into meetings with journalists eager to do features on Harrat Salma, meetings with lawyers and accountants and financiers and surveyors—but Karim still managed to snatch time with Lily.

'I'm sorry, *habibti*,' he said one evening with a sigh, settling her on his lap. 'I would really like to take you out for dinner, but my life seems to have turned into wall-to-wall meetings.'

'It's OK.' She understood. It had been that way for her, when she'd first set up Amazing Tastes.

'No, it's not OK. And I don't want you thinking that I've used you to help with my business and now I'm just using you for sex, because it isn't like that.'

'No, because *I'm* using *you*,' she teased back, wanting to lighten his mood. 'Didn't you realise that you're officially my stud?'

He laughed, then stroked her face, suddenly tender. 'That's one of the things I love about you, Lily. Your sense of humour.'

He'd said it. The L-word. But he hadn't said it in the phrase that Lily secretly wanted to hear him say. A word she wasn't going to beg for. And she had no intention of being the first one to say it.

Oh, Lord.

She was in love with this man.

Really in love.

It hit her like a ton of bricks. What she'd felt for Jeff…that was nothing, compared with this.

She knew she had to mask her feelings. He was only hers temporarily; even if he felt the same, nothing could happen. Not with such a clash of cultures and lifestyles and expectations—and one day soon he'd have to go back to his duty, his destiny. Which meant it was doubly important that he didn't guess how she felt about him, didn't feel the pressure. Life would be hard enough for him, soon, with his time never his own and his whole world given over to duty.

So she simply smiled and kissed him and pretended everything was absolutely fine.

Without even discussing it, they fell into an arrangement: the evenings when she worked, they spent at her house, and the evenings when she didn't, they spent at his flat. And even though Lily tried to tell herself that this was casual and temporary, that she'd manage to protect her heart so it wouldn't turn to dust when it was all over, as the days passed she found herself falling more and more in love with Karim. Growing closer to him.

'So what do you see yourself doing in five years' time?' Karim asked one night, when they were curled up in her bed.

Picking our children up from school, was her first thought. And then she was horrified. Although she was fond of Hannah's little daughter Julie, Lily had never seen herself as broody. And she and Karim weren't in the position to think about having children anyway.

But now the idea was in her head, she could imagine her belly swelling with Karim's child. She could imagine his hands cradling her abdomen and feeling their baby kick. See the love and pride on his face as he held their newborn baby…

No, no, no.

It wasn't going to happen; there was no point in fantasising about it.

'I don't know,' she said, striving for a casual air. 'Probably the same as I do now. Wowing the rich and famous with my food, and writing articles to give others the confidence to cook something spectacular.'

'What about your articles? Have you ever thought about turning them into a book?' he asked.

'Maybe.'

'And you'd be great as a TV chef,' he said, warming to his theme. 'Watching you cook is amazing. I'm never sure whether you remind me more of a dancer or a magician.'

TV chef.

Even the words made her want to scream.

'Lily?' he asked.

'Nothing. Just a bit of a headache,' she fibbed.

He smoothed her hair back from her temples. 'I don't think so—from the look in your eyes just now, I touched a raw nerve. I apologise.'

'It's all right.'

'No, it's not.' He drew her closer. 'You once told me that it's not good to bottle things up. Talk to me, Lily.'

She sighed. 'It's not a pretty story. It's a while ago now, and I'm over it.'

'You were offered a slot, but you ended up with the producer from hell and it didn't work out?' he guessed.

Hardly. She could work with practically anyone. The truth was much, much more sordid. 'No. I was in partnership with someone.' She sighed. 'I might as well tell you the whole thing. And if you despise me for being a fool, so be it.'

'Elizabeth Finch, you're very far from being a fool.' He stroked her face. 'Tell me.'

'Jeff and I…we worked together in a kitchen, and we fell in love. Got married.' She bit her lip. 'Then Jeff suggested that we should set up our own restaurant. It was a challenge, and we worked stupid hours to get it off the ground, but we did it. We were doing well. I thought everything was fine.' How naïve and trusting she'd been. 'One of our regulars was a TV producer and thought he'd be a natural on TV. She was trying to set up a new kitchen series, and she said Jeff had the right touch to appeal to everyone. Her bosses liked the pilot, so she got the green light to do the new show. And it got to the stage where we didn't see that much of each other, because Jeff was at the studios all the time and I was busy running things at the restaurant.' She shrugged. 'I thought that was just the way business goes, and things would start to settle down a bit once production had finished and the show had started airing.'

'But it didn't?'

She blew out a breath. 'No. Because Jeff wasn't at the studios as much as I thought he was. At least, not for the programme.' Even now, the betrayal made her feel sick. 'He was having an affair with the producer.'

Karim held her closer. 'I'm sorry he treated you like that. You deserved a lot better.'

'Turns out I'm a really lousy judge of character,' she said. 'The affair might've blown over—I didn't have a clue about it, so maybe our marriage could've survived that. But I'd also trusted him enough to deal with the financial side of things.' She shook her head in frustration. 'He was my husband, my business partner. Of *course* I trusted him. I could've done the finances myself, but he knew I loved developing recipes and he said he'd take over the financial stuff to give me more time doing what I enjoyed most, especially as he wasn't pulling his full weight in the kitchen and leaving most of the work to me.' She lifted a shoulder. 'I thought he loved me, that he was working for *us*—just as I was.'

'What happened?'

'I got a phone call from the bank about a cheque I'd written to a supplier. It bounced. They said we were overdrawn, and I said we couldn't possibly be—I knew the kitchen was running at a profit.' She closed her eyes. 'It turned out Jeff had emptied our joint account, right up to the limit of the overdraft.'

He stroked her hair. 'Bastard. I hope you took him to court.'

'You can't sue your husband,' she said. 'We had joint liabilities—so that meant I was jointly responsible for the overdraft. And he'd also withdrawn nearly all the money from our savings account. There wasn't a thing I could do about it.' She swallowed hard. 'We sold the business, but obviously there was a mortgage and loans involved. By the time everything was paid off, there was nothing left. Except the overdraft.'

'There must have been some way to make him pay his share—and your half of the money he took.'

'No. He'd used the money as a deposit on a flat. It was in her name, so I couldn't touch it. Believe me, I took legal advice. Hannah found me in tears one morning, made me tell her the whole story and marched me straight to a lawyer.' She sighed. 'If I'd left the overdraft, the interest would've kept mounting up and I could've ended up with a county court judgment against my name. I didn't want that, because then I'd have had real problems getting another mortgage or business loan.'

He swore in Arabic. 'You still could have told a journalist— he was on television, so being a minor celebrity would be enough to make the media interested in what he did. You could have dragged him through the papers and shamed him into paying back what he owed you. Not to mention the fact that the papers would have paid you for your story.'

'And get into a public slanging match?' She shook her head. 'No. I didn't want my name dragged all over the papers, Karim. I didn't want people to remember me as the stupid bimbo whose husband cheated on her and took her to the cleaners— that kind of mud sticks and it isn't good for business.' She paused. 'But I sure as hell won't ever go into business with anyone again. And I'm never, ever, *ever* getting married again.'

'I'm sorry you had to go through such a horrible experience.' He cradled her close. 'It's kismet. What goes around, comes around. He'll get his comeuppance.'

'Right now,' she said, 'he's still doing perfectly fine as a TV chef. Even though he's split up from his producer. Apparently he couldn't stay faithful to her, either.'

'Kismet takes time,' Karim said thoughtfully. 'And he's a very stupid man. Didn't he realise what he had in you?'

'Obviously I wasn't enough for him.'

'More fool him,' Karim said. 'And I know he let you down badly but, *habibti*, believe me, not all men are complete bastards.'

'I know they're not. My dad wasn't. He would've been

turning in his grave if he'd known what a mess he left us in.' The words were out before she could stop them.

'Your dad?' Karim asked.

She'd started telling him. Might as well finish it. 'He died when I was four—it was one of those really unexpected, shocking things.'

'An accident?' Karim guessed.

'He just died, even though he was never ill,' Lily said matter-of-factly. 'Mum says the coroner thought it might have been an undiagnosed heart condition. And he really did love me and Mum. He was never too busy for me when I was little—I remember him doing finger-painting with me and drawing me lots of pictures. But Mum says he was pretty hopeless with money. He never got round to sorting out any life insurance.' She smiled ruefully. 'I suppose his head was too full of his art.'

'He was an artist, too?'

She nodded. 'That's how they met, at art school. They fell in love and got married when they were students, and Mum went into labour with me halfway through her last exam. I wasn't planned, but they loved me anyway and she said there was always going to be room in their life for me. Once they knew they were expecting me, they really wanted to be a family.' She sighed. 'She says Dad would've been a really great artist if he'd lived, but there just wasn't enough time. He never got his big breakthrough.' She looked away. 'We struggled a fair bit. Mum didn't even have enough money to cover the funeral costs.'

Which explained a lot, Karim thought. Lily had had to scrimp and save and make do when she was little—and then do it all over again to make up for the financial mess her ex-husband had left her in. 'Clearly you've worked your heart out for the last few years,' he said.

'Because of the house, you mean?' she asked, guessing instantly what he meant.

'Islington's a nice area. And your house isn't exactly small.'

'It's not actually my house—it's my stepfather's. Well, my sort of stepfather's,' she said awkwardly.

'Sort of?'

'Mum met Yves when I was a teenager. He fell in love with her, but she refused flatly to get involved with him. He bought every single one of her paintings from the gallery, one by one, so she had to talk to him each time; and finally she agreed to let him take her out to dinner. I was really pleased, because it was about time she did something for herself.' She smiled. 'And Yves is gorgeous. He's funny and clever and kind. I'll never forget my dad, but Yves has been there for me for the last twelve years. I think of him as my dad, and Mum really ought to make an honest man out of him.'

'But she's scared in case she loses him?' Karim asked.

Lily shook her head. 'The thing is, Yves owns a vineyard. And he's made a pretty good living out of it.' She bit her lip. 'She says she won't marry him until she's got as much money as he has. I can kind of see her point—she doesn't want people to think she's a gold digger.'

'Even though they've been together twelve years?'

'Even though,' Lily agreed. 'My mum has this independent streak. She refuses to rely on anyone.'

'And you're just like your mother,' Karim said. He'd recognised her refusal to rely on others from the moment he'd knocked on her door.

'Not quite, or I wouldn't be living in his house.' She sighed. 'The way Yves put it, it was an investment. Buying the house gives him a base in London—and in me he has a tenant he can trust to look after the house properly and tell him straight away if any work needs doing.' She wrinkled her nose. 'It was a cooked-up scheme between them to help put me back on my feet. I made them admit it, eventually. But they did it because they love me. And I suppose they do have a point—I needed a decent-sized kitchen for work and there was no way I could've afforded even a studio flat on my own, especially as I'd lost everything I'd worked for including all my savings. But I'm not some spoiled, brat of a daughter who takes it all for granted.' She lifted her chin. 'I pay Yves a fair rent. We had quite a big fight about it, but he accepts that I want to make my own way, not rely on others.'

'So you've been let down by two men you should've been able to expect to support you,' he said quietly.

'Dad didn't do it deliberately.'

He heard what she wasn't saying, and said it for her. 'But Jeff did.'

'He was ambitious. More ambitious than I am.'

'And that's why you don't want to be a TV chef—you don't want to put yourself in competition with him and have it all dragged up?'

'I never wanted to be a celebrity chef in any case. You're setting yourself up as an Aunt Sally—you can't put a foot wrong or make an off-the-cuff remark, or it'll haunt you for the rest of your life. And there's all the personal stuff, too—you get criticised for your wardrobe or your hair or your shape.'

'There's nothing wrong with your wardrobe. Or your hair.' He slid his palm across her curves. 'Or your shape. Especially not your shape.'

'That's not the point. Everyone thinks they have a right to comment about you, and I'm just not interested in being part of all that.'

'And yet you cook for celebs.'

'That's different.' She flapped a dismissive hand. 'I'm not in the limelight. And I happen to like doing what I do now. I know people actually use my recipes because they write in to the magazine, and I love it when they tell me they didn't think they'd ever be able to make something but they could follow my recipes.' She smiled. 'Someone once told me the best revenge is living well, so I'm doing exactly that. I'm working in a business I love, doing what I enjoy, and I can pick and choose my clients. If I'm not happy with the way a client acts towards me, the next time they ask for a booking I might fib about free slots and suggest they use someone else.'

He rubbed the tip of his nose against hers. 'Were you fibbing about free slots when I asked you?'

'No, I really am booked up three months in advance,' she told him.

'But you're not going to let your heart get involved again.'

'Absolutely not.' It was a lie. She already had.

Though she knew it couldn't go further between them. Couldn't be permanent. Wrong culture, wrong life, wrong everything. And even if Karim *could* ask her to be his wife, he'd told her that the women in his family didn't work. Marrying Karim would mean giving up her entire life. Relying on him. Losing her independence, everything she'd worked so hard for during the last four years.

It wasn't going to happen.

She changed the subject swiftly. 'So what about you, then? Where do you think you'll be in five years' time?'

'I already know that. Back in Harrat Salma.' His voice was toneless. 'Eventually my father's going to retire and I'll take his place.'

'And you really don't want to do it.'

'Yes and no,' he answered enigmatically. 'Does it show that much?'

'To me—yes.' She stroked his face. 'You're bottling it up, Karim. It's not good for you.'

Karim thought about it. She was right. And she'd told him a confidence. So maybe he could tell her the things he'd never told anyone else, even his best friend.

'Do you have a younger brother or sister who could take over and let you go back to doing the vulcanology stuff?' she asked.

He frowned. 'I thought you looked me up on the Internet?'

'I did, but I didn't snoop. I just learned who you were and that you spent a lot of time at parties,' she said lightly. 'Though I know now the serial party-boy bit isn't strictly true.'

'I have a younger sister,' he said, 'Farah. She's four years younger than I am.'

'And is she the sort who'd be happier running the country?'

'No.' He sucked in a breath. 'Even if she was, it isn't an option—because of the current laws of succession.'

Her eyes glittered.

'I know, you're Western-born, you have a different take on things,' he said, 'and I agree with you on this point. One of the things I will change is the succession laws. My father and grandfather have taken a modern approach in that women in Harrat Salma have the right to an education and the freedom to do any job they choose, but they don't have to do it if they don't want to. If they want to stay home and care for their family, then that is an option too. And I don't see why men can't take on that role too, should they choose.'

She smiled. 'Now that's forward thinking—few men do that, even here.' She paused. 'What would happen if you didn't rule?'

'The title would pass to a cousin. But that's a cop-out, Lily. It's my burden. I need to accept it and find a way of meshing my heart with my duty.'

She dropped a kiss on his chest, in the region of his heart. 'I'm sorry. But, as the oldest, you must have grown up knowing that this would happen?'

'No.' He looked away. 'Because I wasn't always the oldest.'

CHAPTER TWELVE

SHE stared at him, not quite understanding. 'You what?'

'I wasn't the always oldest,' Karim repeated. 'I was the middle child.'

So the fact he was the oldest now meant that tragedy had scarred his past. He'd lost his older brother.

Lily knew that if she asked questions now, pushed him to tell her about it, he'd clam up. Instead she shifted so that his head was pillowed on her breasts, wrapped her arms around him and waited for him to speak.

'I had a brother. Tariq. He's—he *was*,' he corrected himself sharply, 'four years older than I am. Very quiet and serious— everyone was always telling him he needed to have some fun before he took on running the country.'

Just as the media thought Karim was doing. The ultimate playboy, privileged and spoiled, frittering his time away while he waited to become ruler of his country. Expecting it all to be handed to him on a plate.

How little they knew.

'And eventually one of my cousins persuaded him to go dune-bashing. Except their buggy overturned. And they weren't experienced enough to get the car out of the dune before it sank into it. He suffocated in the sand.'

Her heart contracted. What a terrible way to die. And how

hard it must have been for those left behind, for those who'd told him to go and have fun—they must all have felt so guilty, as if they'd pushed him to his death.

No wonder Karim was so set against the idea of tourists going dune-bashing—the activity that had killed his brother.

'When did it happen?' she asked softly.

'Five years ago. It's strange to think I'm a year older now than he ever was.'

She didn't know what to say. Words weren't enough. So she simply held him.

'I couldn't believe it when my father called to tell me the news. Nobody could believe it.' He swallowed hard. 'I went straight home. And even as I walked in I was expecting to see Tariq sitting where he usually did, quietly reading. He wasn't there. Just an empty space.' He pressed a kiss against her skin. 'I still find it hard walking into the palace. And how much worse it must be for my parents and my sister, having to live with it every day.' He grimaced. 'Farah's name means "Joy". And she is a joy—I've loved her ever since the minute my mother first introduced me to my new baby sister. But since Tariq died, she's become so quiet and withdrawn. I worry about her.'

'And she probably worries about you. You're trying to cram every minute with work and partying, so you don't have time to think about your brother—except that all the partying's really a façade for work,' Lily said gently. 'Do you think that's what your parents really want for you?'

'There is no other choice. I have to step into Tariq's shoes.' He closed his eyes. 'That's why I gave up my PhD.'

He'd been studying for a doctorate? She'd realised he was clever. He could've reached the very top of his chosen profession. And yet he'd walked away from it to do his duty. He'd done the right thing by his family and his country, even though it was breaking his heart. She stroked his hair. 'For what it's worth, I think you'll make an excellent ruler. Because you listen.'

'I'll make a good ruler,' he said, 'because I would never dishonour my family or my brother's memory by doing otherwise.'

'That's the other reason you work so hard, isn't it?'

He frowned. 'What?'

'Not just to stop yourself missing your brother. To stop yourself missing your dreams.'

'Maybe.' He moved so that he was facing her. 'Nobody else knows about this, Lily.'

She cupped his cheek in one hand. 'I'm not going to betray your trust, Karim. I'm not going to tell anyone.'

'I know.' He turned his face and pressed a kiss into her palm. 'And thank you. For listening and not judging.'

'Isn't there any way you could compromise?'

'No. There is no middle way. And I made the choice freely.'

'Because you couldn't live with yourself if you turned your back on your family when they needed you most.'

'*Habibti*, you're scaring me now,' he said lightly. 'You're reading straight from my heart.'

She understood him. Just as she knew he understood her. And she really, really hoped that right now he couldn't read her heart. That he couldn't read the things she hadn't told him, for his sake. Because now she knew just how strongly he believed in doing his duty, she realised that she couldn't stand in his way.

But there was one way she could tell him. Without words.

She bent her head. Kissed her way along his collarbones and then drew a line of tiny, nibbling kisses along his throat.

Karim shivered and turned onto his back. She smiled against his skin and she worked her way downwards, along the line of his breastbone, down to his navel. She teased him with the tip of her tongue, drawing a complicated pattern on his skin.

He groaned. '*Habibti*, I think I'm about to lose my mind.'

She could guess what he was thinking. Wondering. And that was exactly what she had in mind. 'I've hardly started,' she said. She trailed the ends of his hair against his skin; he gasped and tilted his hips towards her. Smiling, she moved lower and breathed on his erection, and to her delight he actually quivered.

'Lily…you don't ha—' he began.

Oh, yes, she did. She opened her mouth, and closed it over his flesh.

'Oh-h-h,' he breathed, completely forgetting to finish his sentence. His hands slid into her hair, urging her on.

I love you, she said silently. I love you and I know I'm going to have to let you go, but I'm going to make memories with you. And right now I'm going to make you see the desert stars you miss so much.

Karim was muttering now in Arabic as she stroked him, teased him with her lips and her tongue and her fingers until he was completely lost to pleasure. She didn't have a clue what he was saying; she heard her name, and then something she couldn't decipher.

And then her mission was most definitely accomplished.

Telling each other their deepest, darkest secrets marked a turning point in their relationship. Lily was trying desperately to hold back, yet all the time she was falling more deeply in love with Karim. The man who put others first. The man who was strong enough to give up his dreams for his duty. The complete opposite of selfish, faithless Jeff.

And although neither of them spoke again about what they'd discussed, she noticed that Karim seemed to cherish her. As if he, too, knew that their time was limited and they were going to make memories. That every moment was precious. Little moments like an early Sunday morning drive to the beach in Karim's outrageously low-slung car before Lily had to be back to prepare for work, feeding the ducks on the lake at Finsbury Park, watching the sun rise from Karim's balcony.

Karim woke in the middle of the night, his body wrapped round Lily's. Her fingers had become laced with his during sleep; the only way they could've been closer was if his body had eased inside hers.

He pressed his face to her shoulder, breathing in her scent. Funny how it always seemed to calm him. Make him feel centred. Make him feel capable of running the entire world, let alone Harrat Salma.

And then it hit him.

He and Lily had argued about love and marriage. He believed that it was all about trust and respect and honour, and affection would grow. And she—despite the way her ex-husband had wrecked her life—believed in love. Which she'd defined as respect and affection and physical attraction.

That was everything he felt for her.

Respect for the way she ran her business, her independence and her drive. And he liked her as a person, enjoyed her company. Physical attraction—absolutely. She blew his mind, to the point where he actually slept with her as well as had sex with her. Something he'd never let himself do before. Something he'd never really wanted to do before.

And now he knew why.

Because now his heart was involved. He was in love with Lily. He was in love, for the first time in his life.

So much for the ground rules. He'd managed to stick to two of them: he'd been faithful to her and he'd kept work and their relationship separate.

The stumbling block was number one.

Temporary.

Because now Karim knew he didn't want their relationship to be temporary. He didn't want to leave Lily behind in England

and go back to Harrat Salma to marry someone of his parents' choice, the way he'd planned to do. No. Now, he knew he wanted to marry a woman of his *own* choice.

Specifically, he wanted to marry Lily. Because he loved her.

He wanted to spend the rest of his life with her. Help her bring their children up. Share his triumphs and his fears with her.

He wanted her. Needed her. And he was pretty sure she felt the same way, even though she hadn't said a word about it and they were both pretending that everything was just fine and dandy. If he asked her to marry him…would she be his?

Yet how could the heir to the sheikhdom marry a woman like Lily—a woman from a different culture, a woman who ran her own business, a woman who was divorced?

And that raised other issues. Lily had been hurt before. Lost everything. She'd built up her business from nothing, loved what she did. There was no way she could run Amazing Tastes in London from such a distance; and there was absolutely no way she could set up the same kind of business in Harrat Salma. The wife of the heir couldn't be a servant for someone else.

Would she be prepared to give it all up for him?

Karim spent three more days trying to talk sense into himself. Telling himself that giving her up would be the best thing for both of them.

He failed.

Dismally.

And he knew that the only thing he could do now was to face it. Bring everything into the open. And hope that somehow they'd find a way to secure their future. Together.

They'd managed to synchronise their schedules to snatch a morning together and were sitting on Lily's patio, holding hands and watching the butterflies settling on her ceanothus and the bees clustering round the hebe, when Karim's fingers tightened round hers. 'Lily?'

'Yes?'

'I've been thinking.' He paused. 'Our ground rules. I want to change them.'

She went very, very still. Was he telling her that it was over? 'How do you mean?' she asked carefully.

'Exclusive is fine. Keeping work and personal stuff apart is fine. But the first rule…that has to go.'

The first rule was 'temporary'. Her heart missed a beat. Surely he wasn't going to…? No, of course not. He *couldn't*.

'You asked me once what would happen if I fell in love with someone. I said it wasn't going to happen.' He shrugged. 'Seems I'm not always right. I learned something this week. That it could happen. That it *has* happened.' He slid from the chair and knelt on the patio in front of her. 'Lily, I want to marry you. Will you marry me?'

'I…' She couldn't believe he'd asked her that. The one thing she'd secretly wanted him to ask her. The one thing she knew she couldn't have. She so desperately wanted to say yes. But, for his sake, she had to do the right thing. 'I can't.'

'Why not? Your divorce from Jeff was finalised, wasn't it?'

'A long time ago.'

'So you're free. Why can't you marry me?'

'All kinds of reasons.' Did he really need her to spell it out for him? He knew just as well as she did why they couldn't do this. She dragged in a breath. 'Karim, you're royalty. I'm a commoner.'

'That's not an issue, as far as I'm concerned.'

'But it's not just *you* that you have to consider, is it? What about your parents? Your country? Karim, I'm everything you can't marry. I'm not Arabic, I'm not a princess, I work for a living, and I've been married before. I'm as unsuitable as you can get.'

'You suit me.' His eyes crinkled at the corners. 'I'm of sound mind. And I'm quite capable of choosing my own bride. Which is why I'm asking you to marry me—something, I might add, that I've never, ever asked anyone else.'

She shook her head. 'But you *can't*. You've already told me that your parents are arranging a marriage for you. You haven't even mentioned me to your family, have you?'

'No,' he admitted.

'You're the future ruler of Harrat Salma. You have so many things to consider. You can't do just as you like.'

'Actually, *habibti*, as the ruler of Harrat Salma, technically I can do exactly as I like. And I want to marry you.'

He wanted to marry her.

Which meant he felt the same way about her that she did about him.

He hadn't actually said the three little words—he'd skirted round it, saying that he'd fallen in love. But she knew what he meant. He loved her. Just as she loved him.

She ought to be doing cartwheels and whooping. Instead, all she felt was fear. Sickening, rushing fear that this was where everything was going to hit the skids. 'But…you'll be going back to Harrat Salma.'

'Eventually, yes. And there will be a lot of toing and froing between here and there in between,' Karim said.

'So that means you want me to go back with you.'

He rubbed his thumb against the backs of her fingers. 'That's the general idea of marriage, *habibti*—that two people live together and spend their free time together.'

'So I'll be leaving everything here.'

'Not exactly. Your family is in France,' he pointed out. 'And they're very welcome to visit whenever they like. Your friends, too.'

'And my business?'

He blew out a breath. '*Habibti*, I know how I feel about you and I think you feel the same way about me. I don't have a choice about my job, but you have a choice about yours. And some rules I can bend, but the work thing I can't.'

'So you're expecting me to give up my independence.'

Everything she'd worked for. Everything she'd relied on, since Jeff.

'I know it's a lot to ask.'

Did he? He was used to everything falling onto a plate for him. 'Yes, it really is a lot to ask. Especially as you can't guarantee that your family or your people will accept me.'

'Rafiq likes you.'

'That's different. He's over here; he knows me as your cook and he probably guessed a long while ago that I'm sleeping with you. Accepting me as your wife would be a whole different kettle of fish.' She paused. 'OK. Let's put it the other way round. Would you give up everything for me, stay here with me?'

His eyes darkened. 'I don't have a choice in the matter. You do.'

'But if you had a choice,' she persisted.

'If I had a choice, yes,' he agreed. 'But I don't have the luxury of choice. You'd be asking me to choose between you and my family.'

'And you're asking me to give up everything I've built up over the years. For you.'

'Are you worried that I'm going to betray you, the way Jeff did—that I'm going to let you down?' Karim shook his head in seeming disbelief. 'Haven't you learned anything about me, these past few weeks? I've trusted you with things I've told nobody else. I've shared things with you that I've shared with nobody else. Doesn't that tell you anything?'

'Of course it does. But, Karim, you're not free to ask me to marry you, and you know it. You're living in a fantasy world.' One she so badly wanted to share. But it wasn't going to happen and they had to face facts.

He glared at her, clearly about to argue with her when the doorbell rang.

Coward that she was, she was glad that it stopped him saying something unforgivable. Stopped her saying something just as irrevocable. 'I'd better get that,' she said, and rushed from the garden before he could protest.

To her surprise, Rafiq was at the door, looking strained. 'Is Karim with you?' he asked.

'Yes.'

'*Al hamdu lillah,*' he said, sounding relieved.

'You'd better come in. What's happened?'

Karim, clearly having heard a snatch of the conversation, was already heading towards them. 'Rafiq? What is it?'

'I've been trying to get hold of you for the last hour. Your mobile phone was switched off.' Rafiq glanced at Lily. 'So was yours. And you didn't answer your landline.'

Now he'd said it, she looked at the phone and she could see the light flashing, telling her that she had a message. 'Sorry. We were sitting in the garden. We didn't hear the phone,' she apologised.

'I hoped that was the case. Because if you hadn't been here…'

'What's *happened*?' Karim asked again, and this time there was a regal note in his voice. A demand that his question should be answered.

'Your father. He's in hospital.'

'*What?*' Karim's face paled.

'He's had a heart attack. Your mother is with him, and she said to tell you that the worst is over. That he will recover.'

A muscle flickered in Karim's cheek. 'I need to be there.'

'Of course you do,' Lily said.

'I took the liberty of booking a plane ticket and bringing your passport,' Rafiq said. 'The car's outside. We can go straight to the airport.'

Karim looked at Lily, clearly torn.

'Go,' she said. 'We'll finish our discussion later. Go and see him for yourself.'

'Lily.' He held her close, resting his forehead against hers. 'Thank you for understanding.'

'I'd be the same if it was my mum. Go. Ring me when you can and let me know how things are.' Though she had a pretty good idea what this meant. That Karim would have to hand over the job he'd been doing to someone else, and stay in Harrat Salma to take over from his father. Maybe just until his father was better...but maybe for ever.

And she'd have to give him up.

With supreme effort, she kept her voice steady. Calm. Supportive. Even though she wanted to yell and cry and scream and tear her hair out. 'And if you need anything—anything at all—you call me, OK?'

He swallowed hard. 'Thank you, *habibti*.' He kissed her lightly—and then he was gone.

Karim sat on the plane, staring bleakly out of the window. This felt just like the last time, when he'd gone home to Harrat Salma from England after a frantic phone call. When he'd gone home to do his duty. When he'd gone home to find his beloved older brother dead.

This time...would it be the same? Would his father's condition have worsened while Karim flew halfway across the world? Would he make it back in time?

Eight hours. A lot could happen in eight hours. Plus the travelling time from Lily's to the airport, and from the airport to the hospital. He felt sick. Please, let his father hold on.

He wished he'd asked Lily to come with him. To be by his side. For her quiet strength to flow into him, bolster him while he faced his deepest, darkest fears.

But he knew it would have been unfair to ask her. She had commitments. He couldn't expect her to drop everything for him—to let her clients down, break all her promises, lose her integrity. And besides, he needed to talk to his family about her, first. Though this really wasn't the right time.

The plane journey felt as if it took for ever. But there was an official car waiting at the airport, a silent and respectful driver who took him straight to the hospital. He sent Lily a text that he'd arrived safely at Harrat Salma, then switched off his phone as he walked into the hospital.

His mother and sister were there in his father's room. He hugged them both, letting them know his strength would be there to carry them, then sat beside his father's bedside and took his hand.

'My son. You came.' The older man made an effort to smile.

'Of course. The second I heard.' Karim squeezed his father's hand. 'How are you feeling?'

'I've felt better,' Faisal said dryly. 'But they say I'm on the mend.'

'He overdoes things,' Johara said, thinning her lips.

Karim smiled at his mother. 'Just as he's done for at least the last thirty-five years.' But his father's illness was a reminder to all of them that Faisal was getting old. That he was reaching the age where he should hand over the running of the kingdom to his son—or risk working himself to death. If he had another heart attack, he might not be so lucky next time.

'Forgive me,' Faisal said softly.

'There's nothing to forgive. But you need to rest, *Abuya*. And do what the doctor tells you.' Karim hugged his father. 'I'm just glad you don't look as bad as I expected.'

But his father still looked bad enough to worry him.

He was definitely going to have to come home for good. This was his burden, and he'd agreed to accept it five years ago.

He just hadn't expected it to be so heavy. Or to happen quite so soon.

And the idea of having to face all this without Lily…

For his family's sake, Karim kept his feelings to himself. He spent the rest of the evening at the hospital, and returned to the palace with his sister, Farah; his mother, as he'd half expected, refused to leave Faisal's side. He sat talking to Farah, reassuring her that everything was going to be just fine—even though it didn't feel it—and it was nearly three in the morning when he was finally on his own. He glanced at his watch. His country was only two hours ahead of Lily's...but she'd still be asleep by now. It wasn't fair to disturb her.

On the other hand, she'd told him to ring her when he could. She might be lying there, unable to sleep, worrying despite the text he'd sent her. And there was always the chance that the text hadn't arrived. The system wasn't infallible.

He picked up his mobile phone and called her.

She answered immediately. 'Karim? How is your father?'

'A bit sore and a bit subdued. I talked to the doctors, and they say he's on the mend. But I'm going to have to stay here for a while, *habibti*.'

'Of course you are. Your family comes first. Is there anything I can do for you, here?'

'No. But thank you for asking.' And trust her to put him first. He paused. 'It's good to hear your voice, Lily. I miss you.'

'Uh-huh.'

Non-committal. That wasn't good. She was already withdrawing from him. Trying to do what she thought was the right thing, perhaps?

He couldn't face that.

He wanted her. Needed her. *Loved* her. Life without her would be unthinkable. Unbearable. 'Lily?'

'Yes?'

'I might be miles away, but I need you to know one thing. Something I should've told you before I left. Something I meant to do but I made a mess of it—I suppose because I've never done it before. I love you, Lily,' he said softly.

There was a tiny noise at the other end of the line that sounded suspiciously like a sob.

'*Habibti*, are you crying?'

'No-o.'

That wasn't true, and he knew it.

'Karim, I...' This time, he heard her gulp back the tears. 'I love you, too.'

'Everything's going to be all right,' he told her. Though he knew it was an empty promise. Because without her beside him, nothing felt right.

'Sleep, now. I'll call you tomorrow. I love you.'

'I love you, too,' she whispered.

He cut the connection and looked up at the desert stars. The stars he'd missed so much in London. In a heartbeat, he would've traded the light pollution of London for this and never seen the stars again, if it meant that he had Lily.

'There has to be a way for this to work,' he told the stars. 'There *has* to be.'

And he'd go to the ends of the earth to find it, if need be.

CHAPTER THIRTEEN

BEING apart from Karim was hell, Lily found. Even though he called her every night, even though they sent each other texts and emails and tried to pretend everything was absolutely fine, absolutely normal—it was hell. He'd talked about there being an empty space in the palace, after his brother died. Now she knew exactly what he was talking about, because there was an empty space in her life, too. She missed Karim like crazy.

Her longing for him grew worse still on the day that Monica, her editor at *Modern Life*, sent her an early proof of the article—along with a note scribbled on the bottom of Karim's photograph, 'Who IS this gorgeous man?'

The love of my life, she thought. That's who he is. The man who loves me all the way back. And we can't have each other, because he has to go home and rule his country and take a fitting bride to be his sheikha, his queen.

Just as Hayley had promised, Karim looked fantastic, sitting there in her garden, licking gooseberry fool from a spoon. And Lily could remember every single second of that day. When he'd told her what he'd fantasised about during the photographic shoot. When he'd told her to trust him.

She trusted him.

But she couldn't see how they could make their relationship work. There was too much in the way.

With every day that passed, it got worse. And when her Sunday client croaked down the phone to her on the Saturday afternoon, saying that she'd picked up a viral throat infection and she was sorry but she had to cancel the dinner party, Lily knew exactly where she wanted to be.

Being with Karim wasn't an option—there was too much going on in his life right at that moment and he really didn't need the extra pressure of her being clingy—but there was someone she could talk to, someone who'd understand. She picked up the phone. 'Mum? Can I come and see you for a couple of days?'

'Of course, darling. When were you thinking of coming?'

'Tomorrow morning?' Lily suggested hopefully.

'Let me know when your plane's due in, and I'll meet you at the airport.'

Another phone call, along with her credit card, sorted out the ticket; and the fact she was escaping for a few days got her through the evening's work for a dinner party that went on much later than she'd expected.

Though it was good to be busy, because it meant she didn't have time to fret about Karim. His texts and emails and phone calls just weren't enough. And soon they would have to stop, too—when he realised that she was talking sense, that she couldn't marry him and he'd have to marry a suitable bride.

How was she going to face the rest of her life without him? *How?*

She packed the bare minimum of things that night in a flight bag—not wanting to be held up waiting for her luggage to be taken off the plane and knowing that, if necessary, she could borrow clothes from her mother—and caught the early morning flight from Gatwick to the airport at Marseille Provence. She'd texted her mother with her flight details, and to her relief the flight was on time. The second she was through Customs, she looked round for her mother; she could see Amy waving in the corner, and simply ran to her. It had been too, too long since she'd seen her mother.

Amy greeted her with a warm hug; and then, to Lily's horror, she found herself bursting into tears.

'Oh, darling. Whatever it is, it can't be that bad,' Amy soothed.

Oh, yes, it was.

'Come on. Let's go to the car—we'll be on our own and you can tell me everything.'

Lily cried all the way to the car. And for a good fifteen minutes before she could speak and finally tell her mother all about Karim. Everything. Including the marriage proposal that she'd refused.

'Why did you turn him down?' Amy asked, looking completely bemused.

'Not because I want to,' Lily explained. 'I have to. It's the right thing.'

'I still don't see it. Sweetheart, I know you had a horrible experience with Jeff, but it doesn't mean it'll be like that next time round.'

Lily shook her head. 'Karim's an honourable man. He's nothing like Jeff.'

'So why refuse him?'

'Because…' She dragged in a breath. 'Lots of reasons.'

'Such as?' Amy probed.

'Mum, it's hard enough without talking about it.'

'Actually,' Amy said, stroking Lily's hair back from her face, 'I think you'll find it's easier if you do talk. Because sometimes you need someone else's view to show you how things really are—and that they're not as bad as you fear.'

'They're bad, all right,' Lily said with a sigh. 'He's a sheikh, Mum. How can I possibly marry him? I'm not royal-born, I'm from a different culture, and I'm divorced. I'm not an acceptable wife.'

'And you know that for sure, do you? You've met his family and they've all threatened to disown him if he so much as speaks to you again?'

'Well—no,' Lily admitted. 'But I can't go to meet his family. His father's been taken ill and he's been called back to run the country. I don't know when he'll be back or when things will settle down.'

'Have you spoken to him?'

A tear trickled down her cheek. 'Every day. And it's so hard, Mum. I want to do the right thing, for his sake. I can't make him choose between me and his country.'

'Perhaps,' Amy said, 'you don't have to. If he loves you as much as you love him, then follow your heart and you won't go wrong.'

'It's not just his family and his country. Even if that works out and I'm allowed to marry him, I won't be able to work. I've spent four years building up Amazing Tastes. I don't want to throw all that away. I don't want to be dependent on him.'

Amy looked thoughtfully at her daughter. 'Like I was dependent on your father, you mean?'

Lily lifted her chin. 'Yes. And you refuse to be dependent on Yves.'

'Yves. Ah.'

Lily caught the hesitation in her mother's voice. 'Mum? Is everything all right?'

'Ye-es.'

'But?'

Amy simply held out her left hand. On her third finger, a single solitaire sparkled in the sunlight.

Lily simply stared. This was the last thing she'd expected. 'You're engaged? You're actually going to marry him?'

Amy nodded. 'I was going to call you today anyway, and tell you. I was going to ask if we could come over and stay for a couple of days and celebrate properly with you.'

'It's your house—you don't have to ask.'

'Only in name. We think of it as yours,' Amy said.

Lily, knowing this was an argument she couldn't win, simply evaded it. 'And of course I want to celebrate with you. I'm thrilled for you.'

'But?' Amy asked.

'But you've always been so adamant that you wouldn't get married again.'

Amy shrugged. 'Things are different, now.'

Lily frowned. 'Mum? What aren't you telling me?'

'You know I love you, don't you?' Amy's grey-blue eyes were serious.

'Of course I do. And I love you. You know that. But you're scaring me, Mum.' Ice slid down Lily's spine. 'What's happened?'

'Everything's fine now.' Amy took a deep breath. 'I had a bit of a health scare, the week before last. A lump.'

'A lump?' The world spun dizzily as Lily took in the implications. 'The week before last? But…' They phoned each other three or four times a week. Texted each other. Didn't let the distance between England and France get between mother and daughter. 'Why didn't you tell me?'

'Because you were busy, love.'

'*Busy?*' Lily shook her head vehemently. 'I'm never too busy for you, Mum. *Ever.*'

'I know. But I didn't want to worry you.'

'I'm worried now.'

'Darling, there was no point in telling you until I'd had the tests and knew what the diagnosis was—whether it was something to worry about or not.'

'Actually, Mum, there was *every* point. I would've been there with you. You know I would've dropped everything to support you.'

'I know you would.' Amy squeezed her hand. 'But I know what your schedule's like and I didn't want to lean on you.

Remember, I have Yves.' She blushed. 'Actually, he was the one who found the lump. And once we'd got over the initial shock, he told me that he was going to book me in with the best specialist, immediately—and he'd pay any costs for the treatment. The way he put it, I'm more important to him than money, and I'm far more important to him than my stubborn English pride.'

Lily could imagine the scene, and smiled through her worry. 'Sounds just like Yves. So, the results?'

'It was a cyst. Completely benign. And I had it removed the same day. It's healing nicely.' Amy smiled wryly. 'It did one thing, though. It made me reassess my priorities. So I proposed to him.'

'*You* proposed to *Yves*?' Lily stared at her mother in surprise—and then grinned. 'Did you go down on one knee?'

'Of course.'

'And what did he say?'

Amy wrinkled her nose. 'He roared at me. Told me I was a stupid, stubborn Englishwoman—that it was his job to propose, not mine, and he was going to ask me every three minutes for the rest of my life until I said yes.'

'Did he?'

'He timed it down to the second.'

'And you said yes.' Lily hugged her. 'Mum, I'm so happy for you. And should you be driving?'

'Yes, sweetheart, I'm perfectly fine. Stop fussing.' Amy rolled her eyes. 'You're as bad as Yves. And why do I have the nasty feeling you're going to gang up on me with him?'

Lily just smiled. And when Amy drove them back to the vineyard, she greeted Yves warmly. 'I'm so pleased my mother has finally seen sense.' She hugged him. 'To be honest, I've thought of you as my father for the last twelve years. But now I can officially call you *Papa*. And I'm so glad.'

'Oh, *chérie*.' Yves shook his head, clearly overcome with emotion.

'Careful,' Amy said, 'you'll have me crying, next.'

'Cry? We have a wedding to plan. And if I'm not doing the catering, there's going to be trouble.'

'You're not doing the catering,' Yves said, recovering himself, 'because you're going to be our bridesmaid. At least, I hope you are.'

'I wouldn't miss it for the world,' Lily said. 'But Amazing Tastes can still do the catering. Hannah and Bea will do it, under my direction.' She smiled. 'It'll be my wedding present to you. No arguments.'

'I think,' Amy said, 'we'd better give in.'

'As our daughter is a chip off the old block, yes,' Yves said, hugging them both. 'Thank you, *chérie*.'

And having a wedding to plan, Lily thought, was just what she needed—to keep her too busy to think about the wedding that wasn't going to happen.

Karim called Lily later that night; they'd agreed that it was easier for him to ring her. Just hearing her voice made him feel better. 'I miss you,' he said.

'Me too, *habibti*.'

He loved it that she'd tried to speak his language. Even though she'd got it wrong, she'd made the effort. For him. 'To me, you'd say *habibi*,' he said softly.

'*Habibi*,' she dutifully repeated. 'So I take it that *auhiboki* would be wrong, too?'

'Yes.' And not just in the way she thought. She couldn't love him. Not after today. 'To me, you'd say *auhiboka*.'

'*Auhiboka, habibi*.'

The words made him catch his breath. So simple.

Why couldn't life be simple? Why couldn't it have been how it was supposed to be—with Tariq as the heir and himself as a vulcanologist? Dr Karim al-Hassan could've married Elizabeth Finch without any problems and been happy. Deliriously happy. His Royal Highness Karim al-Hassan, on the other hand, wasn't free to make the decision. And it was ripping his heart into tiny, tiny shreds.

When he finally put the phone down, he couldn't bring himself to walk into the palace. His boyhood home, the place where he had so many good memories—and yet the place felt like a prison. Everything was topsy-turvy. So he stayed outside, looking up at the stars—stars that weren't even the same as Lily saw, because they weren't in the same hemisphere.

'Karim?' Johara came to sit beside her son. 'Your father's going to be fine, you know.'

'I know.' Karim reached out to take her hand. 'I love you, *Ommi.*'

'And I love you too.' She stroked his forehead tenderly. 'Are you going to tell me what's wrong?'

'I'm fine,' he lied, not wanting to put any pressure on her. His father's illness was hard enough for her, without having to worry about her son as well. Now wasn't the time to talk to her about Lily.

'*Habibi*, I'm your mother. I can tell there's something wrong,' Johara said gently. 'And it's more than the fact you're here and it's hard without Tariq. It's more than the fact that you're working too many hours to fill your time and stop yourself missing your volcanoes.'

'I'm…' He sighed. 'You're right. I'm not fine. But it's not fair to burden you.'

'Who else are you going to talk to, *habibi*? Your father?'

'Not when he's ill and needs to rest.'

'Then talk to me, *habibi*. Maybe I can help.'

He was silent for a long, long time. Finally, he sighed. 'I met someone in England. Lily. She's…' How could he even begin to describe her? 'She's strong and she's brave and she's quick and she's talented. When she's around, it feels as if the whole room's full of light.'

'You're in love with her.'

It was a statement rather than a question. He nodded.

'Does she feel the same about you?' Johara asked.

'Yes.'

'Ah.' She paused. 'Your father and I, we have been nego-tiating to find you a suitable bride. A woman of royal blood, an Arabic princess who can support you when you take over from your father.'

Karim dragged in a breath. 'I know. And I was prepared to follow our traditions—I wanted a marriage like you and my father have. A marriage with a partner I can trust and respect and grow to love.'

'But?'

He shook his head. 'I can't do that now. Not now I know what it's like to love Lily. I can't make those promises, knowing that I'm lying to my bride and I'm lying to my country and I'm lying to myself. It would feel…dishonourable. *Wrong.*'

Johara looked thoughtful. 'You've spent half your life in England. It's hardly surprising that the culture has rubbed off on you. And other rulers have married women from the West. Maybe the problem isn't so insurmountable.'

Karim closed his eyes briefly. So near, and yet so far.

'I haven't told you everything, *Ommi*. She's divorced. *Not* her fault,' he said. 'I won't break her confidence, but I'd quite like to break her ex's jaw.'

'Violence solves nothing,' Johara said softly.

'I know.' He looked at his mother. 'I'll lead Harrat Salma well.'

'Of course you will, *habibi*. You're a good man. A strong man. But you think you'll lead our country better if she's by your side.'

He bit his lip. 'I asked her to marry me. She refused.'

Johara arched one eyebrow. 'And yet you say she loves you?'

'Yes. And that's why she turned me down. She doesn't think she'll be accepted here as my wife. She's not royal-born, she's not Arabic, and she's divorced.' He sighed. 'I've argued with her about it. And she says I've already made too many sacrifices—she won't let me throw them all away on her.'

'You told her about your volcanoes?' Johara sounded surprised.

'She understands. It's the same with her cooking—she cooks,' he explained. 'She changed her schedule for me, worked stupid hours so she could help me with the business meetings. She made food like you would not believe.' He grimaced. 'Except obviously as my wife she couldn't continue to run her business—she'd be needed in a diplomatic role, by my side.'

'So you're asking her to give up everything,' Johara said thoughtfully. 'Her home, her family, her friends, her career. Her whole life. To live hundreds of miles away, in the public eye, in a place where she thinks the people will not accept her. It's a lot to ask of anyone, *habibi*.' She squeezed his hand.

Time to bite the bullet. Karim looked straight at his mother. 'You know I wouldn't willingly hurt my family. But I need to know…would you accept her?'

Johara said nothing, clearly weighing things up in her mind. And her next words surprised him. 'I guessed there was someone. I can always tell when you've just called her.'

He felt his eyes widen. 'How?'

'Because, just for a little while, there's a smile in your eyes.' She paused. 'As the ruler of our country, you will have many responsibilities. Many burdens. And the woman you've just described to me is not a suitable bride.'

He knew that his mother was speaking on behalf of his father, too. That they would be as one in their decision.

So help him, he'd have to learn to live with it. Live half a life, for the rest of his days. He wouldn't marry—if he couldn't have Lily, he didn't want to share his life with anyone—but he would be a good ruler. Bury himself in his duty. And he'd pray that Lily would find the happiness he so wanted to give her himself but knew he couldn't.

And then he realised that his mother was still speaking. '*Ommi*? I'm sorry. I was miles away.'

'I know.' She stroked the hair back from his forehead. 'I was saying, you need a wife who can support you, who will put a smile in your eyes when the days are hard. And if your Lily can do that for you then, regardless of her background, she is the kind of woman I will welcome as my new daughter.'

He couldn't quite believe what he was hearing. 'You'll accept her?'

Johara inclined her head. 'I'm not saying it will be easy. There will be talk, there will be mutterings. She'll need to compromise on a few things, learn some of our ways. But if we accept her, then our people will, too. They will learn to love her as you do.'

'One hurdle down,' Karim said softly.

'And yet so many more to go?' Johara asked perceptively.

He looked at her in surprise. 'It shows that much?'

'I know you,' she said. 'But if your Lily loves you, she'll see that your destiny involves more than one person's life. And she'll support you in that. She will be beside you all the way.'

'Like you've been to my father?'

'Exactly so,' Johara said. 'Would it help if I talked to her?'

'Probably not,' Karim said. 'Right now, I can't see a way forward.'

'I think,' Johara said, 'you need to go back to England. Talk to her. Show her what's really in your heart. And if it's your destiny to be together, you'll both know it.'

Karim squeezed her hand. 'It'll have to wait. You need me here.'

'We can manage without you for a couple of days. Follow your heart,' Johara advised him. 'And you have a good heart, my son. It won't lead you wrong.'

CHAPTER FOURTEEN

FOLLOW his heart.

The problem was, Karim thought, his heart was torn. Half of him wanted Lily. So desperately. Especially now he knew that his family wouldn't stand in his way.

Yet the sensible half of him knew that he was being unfair, that he couldn't expect Lily to give up her entire life for him.

He was going to have to do the right thing by her. He was going to have to say goodbye. But he didn't want to do it over the phone. He wanted to tell her, face to face—that he loved her more than anything, and that was why he was giving her her freedom.

So he called her. '*Habibti*? I'm on my way back to England.'

'When?'

'My flight gets in this evening.'

'Then I'll meet you at the airport.'

He knew he should refuse politely. But, so help him, he needed to see her. Needed to breathe her scent. Missing her was a physical ache in his gut. So he told her the flight time.

'But don't meet me in your van. I'll call Rafiq and tell him to sort out the insurance for my car.'

'You'd let me drive your car?'

He laughed. 'It's just a box on wheels, *habibti*.'

'It's a top-marque roadster, Karim,' she corrected.

'Whatever,' he drawled.

'But supposing I end up denting it when I park?'

'It's a lump of metal, *habibti*. It'll mend.' He couldn't care less about a scratch on his car, as long as she was all right. 'And anyway, you won't dent it. You're used to parking in tight spaces. You do it all the time.'

'In my van. Not in a high-performance car.'

'Which happens to be a little more comfortable than your van.' Though when it came to discomfort, he knew he'd walk barefoot over burning desert sands to be with her again.

'I love you, Lily,' he whispered. And he knew he'd never stop loving her. 'And I'll be with you soon.'

Soon?

His flight alone would take eight hours.

And every second would feel as if it were wading through treacle.

Lily kept an eye on the arrivals board in the airport lounge. Please don't let the flight be delayed. Please. It had been so long—she could hardly wait these last few minutes.

And then at last she saw Karim walking through Customs. Like her, he'd travelled with only hand luggage to avoid the wait at the other end of the flight. He was dressed casually, in a black, long-sleeved round-neck T-shirt with the sleeves rolled partway up his arms, black jeans and dark glasses. He clearly hadn't shaved since the previous day. And she'd never seen any man look so utterly edible.

She couldn't wait any longer. She just ran to him. And then his arms were round her, holding her tightly, and his mouth was jammed over hers, kissing her as if he'd been gone for a thousand years.

It had felt like a thousand years.

'Lily. I've missed you,' he murmured when he finally broke the kiss. His fingers tangled with hers. 'I hope you've parked nearby. And I'll drive.'

'You've been travelling for what, eight hours? *I'll* drive,' she corrected.

He grinned. 'So you like driving my car, do you?'

'Who wouldn't? And, just so you know, I haven't scratched it.'

'I told you that you wouldn't, O ye of little faith.'

As they walked to the car Karim felt his tensions drop away. The ache of missing her vanished. Just being with Lily made him feel complete, rested. All the same, he indulged her. Let her play at being his driver. Because he knew the conversation they would have to have was going to hurt her, just as it was going to rip his heart into two.

'So where are we going?' she asked. 'Your place or mine?'

'Doesn't matter.'

'Mine, then,' she said decisively.

Probably for the best, he thought. Because at least then she'd be home safely. And he would be the one to walk—well, drive—away.

He wanted to touch her. So badly. He wanted to strip that pretty little camisole top off her, unsnap her jeans, rip off her underwear and lose himself in her soft, sweet body, hot and hard and urgent. He wanted to hear those little incoherent cries she made when she came. He wanted to see her eyes go unfocused. To see her mouth swollen with passion and his kisses.

Though he knew that wouldn't be fair to her. Not when they had this conversation to go through. He couldn't just use her and discard her. So he forced his libido to back down. While she was driving, it was easy: his common sense told him that he couldn't distract her attention from the road, and besides he had to text his mother and Rafiq to let them know he was back in London.

But he found it a lot more difficult when Lily parked the car in the space a few feet away from her gate and handed the car keys back to him. His fingers brushed against hers and his temperature went up several notches. Crazy how just a little, casual touch could get him so hot and bothered.

And it was even tougher when Lily dropped her front door keys, bent down to pick them up, and the curve of her buttocks brushed against his thigh.

Karim was shaking with the effort of not touching her when he finally closed her front door behind them.

'Have you eaten?' she asked.

'I'm not hungry.' All too true. The airline food had tasted like ashes and he'd left most of it. He knew that even one of Lily's fabulous concoctions would taste bad, right now: nothing could get rid of the vile taste in his mouth. The guilt. The misery.

'Lily, we need to talk.' He gestured towards her conservatory sofa.

Without a word, she went to sit down. He sat opposite her, knowing that if he touched her just once he wouldn't be able to go through with this. 'Lily.' He dragged in a breath. 'I've missed you like hell. And being away from you has made me realise how much I love you—no, let me finish,' he said, putting up a hand to ask her not to speak. 'This is hard enough to say.' There was a lump in his throat the size of Vesuvius. 'I talked to my mother about you.'

'I understand.' Lily folded her hands in her lap. 'I told you I wouldn't be an acceptable wife.'

'Actually, no. I told her about you. How I feel about you. She says it won't be easy, but she'd accept you and the rest of Harrat Salma would follow suit.' He bit his lip. 'But she also said something else. She made me realise how much I'm asking you to give up. Your home, your family, your career—your whole life. And I know from talking to Luke that when you build something up from nothing, it's a part of you and it's impossible to let go.' He dragged in a breath. 'I want you to be happy, Lily. I can't be that selfish, to ask you to give up everything for me. So tonight I want to say goodbye. To let you walk away with all my love, and my blessing for the future. And I hope you find someone who deserves you.' His voice cracked. 'Someone who'll love you as much as I do but doesn't have all the complications.'

She was silent for a long, long time.

Well, he could understand that. He didn't exactly feel like talking, himself.

'I'll go now, *habibti*,' he said softly.

'What if,' Lily asked as he stood up, 'I don't want to walk away?'

He stared at her, not quite understanding. 'What?'

'I said,' she repeated, 'what if I don't want to walk away?'

'You have to.'

'No.' She stood up, too. 'You're not the only one who talked to your mother.'

This wasn't sinking in. Maybe the pain of losing her had made him completely stupid. 'You talked to my mother? When?'

'Not yours. *Mine*.' Lily's eyes were very clear. 'And she told me to follow my heart.'

Just what his own mother had said to him.

His heart skipped a beat. Was she saying…?

'And my heart lies with you, Karim.' Then she added the two words he'd taught her from his own tongue, just in case he hadn't got the message. '*Auhiboka, habibi*.'

She loved him.

'Lily.' Her name was a whisper. And then he cracked. Was at her side in nanoseconds. Swept her into his arms and kissed her thoroughly, a deep, hot, powerful kiss right from the centre of his being.

He wasn't aware of carrying her up the stairs to her bed. He had no idea who took whose clothes off or when or where or how. All he was aware of was the feel of her skin against his, her sweet scent, the brush of her hair against his face, the taste of her mouth under his. And then finally his body was easing into her, making them one. The ultimate closeness he'd craved so badly since he'd gone back to Harrat Salma.

With every thrust, he was giving her all that he was. And he could see in her eyes that she understood. That she accepted. That she was giving him just as much back.

And when his climax hit him, it felt as if the desert stars were shimmering above them, with the constellations rearranged to spell her name.

Later—much later—Lily was lying in his arms, her head pillowed against his shoulder, and his fingers were tangled through her hair.

'I've been thinking,' he said.

'Provided it's not the sort of thinking that led you to that ridiculous conclusion about giving me up,' Lily said, her voice slightly tart.

He laughed. 'You admitted that you were thinking along the same lines. About being noble. That's why you held back.'

'Not any more.' She pressed a kiss into his chest. 'And I want at least three more orgasms tonight.'

He felt his penis stir. 'Is that an order?'

'What are you going to do about it?'

'Make you come,' he said, and stole a kiss. 'After we've talked. Anyway, as I said, I've been thinking. Being a princess is going to drive you crackers.'

'You're offering to give it up for me?' She shook her head. 'No, Karim. Because what you do with your life affects your people, your country. I can't deprive them of that.'

Just how his mother had said she would react. Pleased, Karim drew her closer. 'That's not what I had in mind. But I won't ask you to give up everything for me, either. You're used to running a business. Making decisions. And doing what I want for the country—developing it in the right way, bringing prosperity to my people and keeping their lives peaceful and happy—is more than a one-person job.'

She traced circles on his skin with her fingertips. 'So what are you suggesting?'

'That we take joint responsibilities,' he said. 'In things that interest you. Obviously you can't set up another company like Amazing Tastes, but maybe you can share the responsibility of developing tourism with me. Doing something with fusion cooking. Talking to journalists. You could still do your cookery articles. Maybe write a book. Teach the world about the cuisine of my country—*our* country.'

'I'd like that,' she said. 'Though I was also thinking about taking some time off.'

'Time off?'

'You once told me that women also had the right not to work. That if they chose, they could take on a very important role—that of parent.'

He sucked in a breath. 'You're saying that's a role you want?'

'As well as working beside you,' she said. 'That's when I realised I was in love with you.' She gave him a serious look. 'I knew I was in trouble when I actually imagined my belly growing big with your child. I'd never, ever fantasised about being pregnant before.'

'Mmm.' He splayed one hand across her abdomen. 'You've just put the most beautiful picture in my mind. You all warm and round and incredibly sexy.'

'And if we have a son,' she said, stroking his face, 'then we'll call him Tariq.'

'I'd like that.' His voice caught. 'Lily Finch. I love you to distraction. But we seem to have skipped a couple of steps.'

'Skipped?'

'Later, *habibti*. Right now, all I want to do is go to sleep, with you in my arms. Then, I'm going to make you come so hard you see stars.' He kissed her, hard, as a show of faith. 'We have a lot of abstinence to make up for.'

'That,' Lily said, 'sounds just about perfect.'

* * *

On Lily's next days off, they flew to Harrat Salma—via Provence, so Karim could meet his future in-laws and receive their approval. And although Lily's stomach was in knots when the plane landed, knots that tightened even further when the official car drove them to the palace and she followed Karim to be received by his parents, the smile on Johara's face told her that everything would be all right.

'Welcome, my daughter,' Johara said, completely ignoring convention and hugging Lily. 'Welcome to our house. And thank you for taking the shadows from my son's eyes.'

Faisal and Farah were equally welcoming, and all Lily's worries about not fitting in vanished completely. They accepted her for who she was, and she discovered that they loved her already because of Karim. And by the time she went to bed that night—on her own, so as not to shock everyone—she felt as if she'd always been part of Karim's family.

The following day, Karim took her for a stroll in the city, introducing her to the spice market and teaching her the names of everything in Arabic. And in the afternoon he took her on a flight to the far side of the country, and drove them himself in a four-wheel-drive car through a harsh terrain of lava fields, pointing out all the geological features.

Lily had a feeling that she knew exactly what he had in mind. A trip that a certain type of tourist—the type Karim wanted to attract most—would enjoy. But as his eyes were almost pure gold with joy, she didn't say a word; she simply let him show her the wonders of Harrat Salma.

Finally, he parked the car. Helped her up a gentle climb.

She knew exactly what she was looking at when she stared at the crater. 'And you're absolutely *sure* this is extinct?' she questioned.

'Yes, *habibti*. I would never put you in danger,' he reassured her.

When they were on a broad plateau within the crater, he took the contents from his backpack—food, water, and a thick sleeping bag big enough for both of them. They ate a simple cold meal and watched the sun setting. As the temperature dropped Karim wrapped a cloak round her and together they watched the stars emerge in the darkening sky.

'Karim, this is incredible,' she whispered, awed. 'Like nothing I've ever seen. Not even the skies over the lavender fields in Provence match this.'

'Wait,' he told her. 'The best is yet to come.'

And as the moon rose she saw what he meant; the minerals on the inside of the crater glittered in the moonlight. 'Sleeping among the stars, just like you said.'

'I didn't think I'd ever be able to bear coming here again,' he said. 'Knowing that I always intended to lead the tourist expeditions here and everything had changed so I couldn't any more. But tonight…this is for you and me. Something special I can share with you.'

'Something really special.' She was blown away that he'd wanted to share something so spectacular with her.

'You've brought the joy back into my life, Lily. Thank you.'

'You've brought the joy back into my life, too,' she said. 'You've made me realise there's more to life than work. Taught me all about love.'

'As you taught me.' He brushed his mouth against hers. 'Remember I said we'd skipped a couple of steps? I think it's time we rectified that.' He shifted so that he was on one knee before her, and pulled a velvet-covered box from his pocket to reveal a single diamond that flashed fire beneath the moonlight. 'Elizabeth Finch, you're the light of my eyes and the heart of my heart. Will you marry me?'

'Yes,' she said. 'Most definitely yes.'

EPILOGUE

THREE months later, Amazing Tastes held its last important function under Lily's management: catering for the wedding of Amy Finch and Yves Lefebure after the ceremony in the tiny Provençal church. A wedding where Lily was the bridesmaid, but she only had eyes for her escort—tall, dark and utterly gorgeous in a wing-collar shirt, cravat and morning coat— who held her hand tightly all through the ceremony, knowing that soon they'd be making those same vows to each other.

And the month after that saw a much larger wedding in Harrat Salma. One where the whole country celebrated. Particularly when His Royal Highness Karim al-Hassan's very English bride made her wedding vows…and added some words of her own in their tongue when she addressed Karim.

'*Auhiboka. Ya rohi. Ya hayaati. Elal abad.*' I love you. You are my soul. You are my life. Always.

* * * * *

Turn the page for an exclusive extract from

THE PLAYBOY SHEIKH'S VIRGIN STABLE-GIRL
by
Sharon Kendrick

Claimed by the sheikh—for her innocence!

Polo-playing Sheikh Prince Kaliq Al'Farisi loves his women as much as his horses. They're wild, willing and he's their master!

Stable girl Eleni is a local Calistan girl. Raised by her brutal father on the horse racing circuit, she feels unlovable. When her precious horses are given to Sheikh Kaliq she *refuses* to be parted from them.

The playboy sheikh is determined to bed her, and when he realizes she's a virgin the challenge only becomes more interesting. However, Kaliq is torn; his body wants Eleni, yet his heart wants to protect her....

"WHAT WOULD YOU SAY, MY DAUGHTER, if I told you that a royal prince was coming to the home of your father?"

She would say that he *had* been drinking, after all. But never to his face, of course. If Papa was having one of his frequent flights of fancy then it was always best to play along with it.

Eleni kept her face poker-straight. "A royal prince, Papa?" she questioned gravely.

"Yes, indeed!" He pushed his face forward. "The Prince Kaliq Al'Farisi," he crowed, "is coming to my house to play cards with me!"

Her father had gone insane! These were ideas of grandeur run riot! And what was Eleni to do? What if he continued to make such idle boasts in front of the men who were sitting waiting to begin the long night of card-playing? Surely that would make him a laughingstock and ruin what little reputation he had left.

"Papa," she whispered urgently, "I beg you to think clearly. What place would a royal prince have *here?*"

But she was destined never to hear a reply, even though his mouth had opened like a puppet's, for there came the sound of distant hooves. The steady, powerful thud of horses as they thundered over the parched sands. On the still, thick air the muffled beat grew closer and louder until it filled Eleni's ears like the sound of the desert wolves that howled at the silver moon when it was at its fullest.

Toward them galloped a clutch of four horses, and as Eleni watched, one of them broke free and surged forward like a black stream of oil gushing out of the arid sand. For a moment, she stood there, transfixed—for this was as beautiful and as reckless a piece of riding as she had ever witnessed.

Illuminated by the orange-gold of the dying sun, she saw a colossus of a man with an ebony stallion between his thighs that he urged on with a joyful shout. The man's bare head was as dark as the horse he rode and his skin gleamed like some bright and burnished metal. Robes of pure silk clung to the hard sinews of his body. As he approached, Eleni could see a face so forbidding that some deep-rooted fear made her wonder if he had the power to turn to dust all those who stood before him.

And a face so inherently beautiful that it was as if all the desert flowers had bloomed at once.

It was then that Eleni understood the full and daunting truth. Her father's bragging *had* been true, and riding toward their humble abode was indeed Prince Kaliq Al'Farisi. Kaliq the daredevil, the lover of women, the playboy, the gambler and irresponsible twin son of Prince Ashraf. The man it was said could make women moan with pleasure simply by looking at them.

She had not seen him since she was a young girl in the crowds watching the royal family pass by. Back then, he had been doing his military service and wearing the uniform of the Calistan Navy. And back then he had been an arresting young man, barely out of his twenties. But now—a decade and a half on—he was at the most magnificent peak of his manhood, with a raw and beautiful masculinity that seemed to shimmer from his muscular frame.

"By the wolves that howl!" Eleni whimpered, and ran inside the house.

* * * * *

Be sure to look for
THE PLAYBOY SHEIKH'S VIRGIN STABLE-GIRL
by Sharon Kendrick,
available August 2009 from Harlequin Presents®!

HARLEQUIN *Presents*

TWO CROWNS, TWO ISLANDS, ONE LEGACY

*A royal family torn apart by pride and lust for power,
reunited by purity and passion*

THE ROYAL HOUSE *of* KAREDES

Pick up the next adventure in this passionate series!

THE PLAYBOY SHEIKH'S VIRGIN STABLE-GIRL
by Sharon Kendrick, August 2009

THE PRINCE'S CAPTIVE WIFE
by Marion Lennox, September 2009

THE SHEIKH'S FORBIDDEN VIRGIN
by Kate Hewitt, October 2009

**THE GREEK BILLIONAIRE'S INNOCENT
PRINCESS**
by Chantelle Shaw, November 2009

THE FUTURE KING'S LOVE-CHILD
by Melanie Milburne, December 2009

RUTHLESS BOSS, ROYAL MISTRESS
by Natalie Anderson, January 2010

THE DESERT KING'S HOUSEKEEPER BRIDE
by Carol Marinelli, February 2010

Eight volumes to collect and treasure!

HPI2843

HARLEQUIN *Presents*

International Billionaires

*Life is a game of power and pleasure.
And these men play to win!*

BLACKMAILED INTO THE GREEK TYCOON'S BED
by *Carol Marinelli*

When ruthless billionaire Xante Rossi catches
mousy Karin red-handed, he designs a way to save
her from scandal. But she'll have to earn
the favor—in his bedroom!

Book #2846

Available August 2009

Look for the last installment of
International Billionaires from Harlequin Presents!

THE VIRGIN SECRETARY'S
IMPOSSIBLE BOSS
by *Carole Mortimer*
September 2009

www.eHarlequin.com   HPI2846

NIGHTS *of* PASSION

One night is never enough!

*These guys know what they want
and how they're going to get it!*

NAUGHTY NIGHTS IN THE MILLIONAIRE'S MANSION
by **Robyn Grady**

Millionaire businessman Mitch Stuart wants no
distractions…until he meets Vanessa Craig.
Mitch will help her financially, but bewitching
Vanessa threatens his corporate rule: do not mix
business with pleasure….

Book #2850

Available August 2009

**Look for more of these hot stories throughout the
year from Harlequin Presents!**

REQUEST YOUR FREE BOOKS!

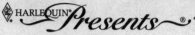 HARLEQUIN® *Presents*®

2 FREE NOVELS PLUS 2 FREE GIFTS!

PASSION GUARANTEED SEDUCTION

YES! Please send me 2 FREE Harlequin Presents® novels and my 2 FREE gifts (gifts are worth about $10). After receiving them, if I don't wish to receive any more books, I can return the shipping statement marked "cancel". If I don't cancel, I will receive 6 brand-new novels every month and be billed just $4.05 per book in the U.S. or $4.74 per book in Canada. That's a savings of close to 15% off the cover price! It's quite a bargain! Shipping and handling is just 50¢ per book*. I understand that accepting the 2 free books and gifts places me under no obligation to buy anything. I can always return a shipment and cancel at any time. Even if I never buy another book, the two free books and gifts are mine to keep forever.

106 HDN EYRQ 306 HDN EYR2

Name   (PLEASE PRINT)

Address   Apt. #

City   State/Prov.   Zip/Postal Code

Signature (if under 18, a parent or guardian must sign)

Mail to the Harlequin Reader Service:
IN U.S.A.: P.O. Box 1867, Buffalo, NY 14240-1867
IN CANADA: P.O. Box 609, Fort Erie, Ontario L2A 5X3

Not valid to current subscribers of Harlequin Presents books.

Are you a current subscriber of Harlequin Presents books and want to receive the larger-print edition? Call 1-800-873-8635 today!

* Terms and prices subject to change without notice. Prices do not include applicable taxes. Sales tax applicable in N.Y. Canadian residents will be charged applicable provincial taxes and GST. Offer not valid in Quebec. This offer is limited to one order per household. All orders subject to approval. Credit or debit balances in a customer's account(s) may be offset by any other outstanding balance owed by or to the customer. Please allow 4 to 6 weeks for delivery. Offer available while quantities last.

Your Privacy: Harlequin Books is committed to protecting your privacy. Our Privacy Policy is available online at www.eHarlequin.com or upon request from the Reader Service. From time to time we make our lists of customers available to reputable third parties who may have a product or service of interest to you. If you would prefer we not share your name and address, please check here. ☐

HP09R

HARLEQUIN *Presents*

Coming Next Month

Plus, look out for the fabulous new collection
Royal and Ruthless from Harlequin® Presents® EXTRA:

HPCNMBPA0709